For The Future

FOR THE FUTURE

John Calvin Harrod

JEP

6 1 39 7 15 5 20 68

ISBN 978-0-6151-7741-0

IAJCHFTF Not a 10-65,
TI Not TX code 37.081,
IA Not Cal. Code 148.3
TRF80

For The Future

Front cover photography by John Calvin Harrod

In the summer of 2000 an obscure journal was found in an undisclosed location. This document records a supposed experiment by the author with time travel. This manuscript has now been made available through the advancement of online publishing. Whether or not the events recorded in this journal are real has yet to be determined.

06/01/00

Dear Calvin,

This may sound very strange from your point of view but please read this letter carefully, and with a sincere trust in my sanity. I need your help. You should receive this letter about four days from today's date. If you haven't heard from me by now then consider this letter our last communication. I need you to come to California and get my notebook.

The book is located in a safe deposit box at _____ Bank in _____ California. I can't tell you what to do with the book; you will have to decide what's best. Inside the safe deposit box you will also find some money to use at your discretion. I assume you've already found the key to the deposit box taped down inside the envelope.

I know it's a lot to ask, and I'm sorry that I can't be more specific, but I promise you will understand all of this when you read the notebook.

You are the only one I can trust. My future depends on you.

Jason Edmond

THE JOURNAL OF JASON EDMOND

~~6/15/99~~
7/15/99

It is just past 1:00 in the morning on the 15th. I bought this notebook a few hours ago at Sav-On's and I can't go to sleep until I write down my first journal entry.

I am sitting by the swimming pool at my apartment complex just writing down a few first thoughts.

My computer broke down a couple of weeks ago so, until I find the funds to replace it, I'll be doing a lot of handwriting, and I think I like it. Writing with pen and paper is very satisfying. It brings back the joy of writing and feels better than just sitting behind a keyboard.

I moved to California in August of 1996 from Austin, Texas, to see what would happen. If I were going to do anything in film, then California would probably be the place to do it. It's been almost three years since I moved out here, and I've gained a lot of experience. Presently I work as a camera salesman at a store in Los Angeles. It's not my goal in life to be a camera salesman, but it keeps me alive while I search for my purpose out here.

This book is a first for me. Writing is not my strongest point, but I'll have to do it if I'm going to prove my experiment. I almost get ahead of myself with the excitement of this whole idea.

7/16/99

Before I get started, I need to explain what I'm doing. Since I don't have to work again until Monday, I'll spend this weekend clarifying as much of this as possible. I'll attempt to condense this stack of notes I've compiled over the last few months and organize them into coherent thoughts. So here goes…

The idea first came to me was while I was taking a script-writing course in college. It was fall, 1995. I began school with a strong influence from my dad to study Physics, but I went a different way and ended up majoring in Radio, Television and Film.

Dr. Simon was my teacher for script-writing class, and he taught it well. Our goal by the end of the semester was to write a screenplay that was between 60 and 120 pages long. The reason for 60 to 120 pages is because the parameters of a screenplay, for the most part, have to match an industry standard. Margins, indentations for dialogue, tab settings for character names, font size, all have to fit those parameters so that it reads at a page a minute. We were supposed to come up with an idea for our story at the first of the semester and slowly build it to a fully developed script.

The first goal was to write a 10-word version of our story, then to extend it to a 100-word version, and next write the same story using 1000 words, minding all along not to use dialogue. Slowly Dr. Simon worked us toward our finished product as he taught us the finer points of character development and plot points. My problem, however, was that I had a fertile and active imagination. Each time a new version of our project was due I had a new story idea, while everyone else was cultivating the same one they had begun with.

Among the several different scripts I gave my teacher, one stuck in my head as a great idea for an experiment. I titled it, "The Hangar Theory." My teacher didn't seem to be enthused by "The Hangar Theory" but, instead, kept asking me to return to my original story, about two downed pilots in the Gulf War. I never went back to the first idea, though now I wish I had. "The Hangar Theory" was left behind and was replaced by several other stories along the way. This "Hangar

Theory" seemed like a great idea to me. It was more like an experiment in Physics than any kind of Hollywood fodder, something that truly needed to be tested. But I saw no way of bringing the idea into reality, so I left it in fiction.

7/16/99

It's still the 16th of July but now it's about 5:00 PM. I had to get out of the apartment for a while and write somewhere else. Right now I'm at Priscilla's Coffee off of Riverside Drive in Burbank, sitting in the back away from everyone and drinking a cup of coffee with cream.

I feel a little anxious about writing in public. With the subject matter of my book being what it is, I find myself looking around, suspicious of almost everyone. Now I'm wondering if some of these people are here to observe me. It might be harder to write here than it was at the apartment. Anyway, here is the story outline for "The Hangar Theory."

On an American military base during the 1940s, just after World War II, General Richardson is overseeing a project that has been initiated by President Harry S. Truman and the post-war military. The military seems to have a lot of energy, but nowhere to go with it. The American government has received word from spies that the Russians are conducting tests on time manipulation and time travel. Counter intelligence reports the tests were only done on the drawing board, but this still sends panic through the halls of Washington.

With a plea from the President of the United States not to fall behind in technology and intelligence, an enormous and possibly dangerous project gets underway. The project is top secret and those working on it are of the highest rank only. Albert Einstein, Robert Oppenheimer, and other great minds are called on to direct the project from closed meetings. "Operation Wells" is tasked with finding the fastest and surest solution to time manipulation and time travel. Slowly, a vision emerges from the "Operation Wells" group.

Herein lies the concept of the experiment and its possibilities. On a military base in New Mexico, an underground hangar is built. It is made to withstand any disaster that could be imagined, and is larger than any structure the military has ever built. It covers two square miles. Inside the hangar, the walls are lined with plaques all reading the same thing; "3:00 PM Central Time, October 12, 1947. The day the doors closed."

At 3:00 PM October 12, 1947, the doors would be closed forever to anyone except those who had created some form of time machine. The theory is that if a time machine were to be made, then only the government could afford such an experiment; therefore, a military base would be the perfect place to conduct tests on time travel. Now if a machine can be made, it may take 100 or maybe even 1000 years to create. And if created, where could it be tested without interfering with the lives of civilians? You take it to the hangar that has stood the test of time.

Now, jump forward 1000 years to the future, where we have created a time machine. We have run tests with the time machine, traveling back one day, one week, two weeks, and returned successfully, all inside the hangar. Now comes the time for a true test. We want to go back to the beginning, back to the founders of the hangar. We, sitting in the year 2947, see the plaque that still hangs on the wall. We hop into our machine, set the clock to match the plaque's time, and press the button. Nothing appears to have happened. We get out to tell our colleagues of our failed attempt when men in archaic military uniforms come running up to us. We have gone nowhere in the hangar but our location in time has changed drastically. But here's the best part, for these gentlemen in 1947 there has been no delay between closing the doors to the hangar and our arrival. It is instantaneous proof of time travel, without much labor for the "Operation Wells" group.

In my screenplay, this is what Einstein and Oppenheimer would have hoped for, instant proof and instant connection to that technology. To coin a modern cliché, "If you build it, they will come."

Why is it so important to have an elaborate underground hangar for time travel? Wouldn't it be easier to go out in the middle of the desert or on a military tarmac and conduct the experiment there? Landmarks, structures, animals, vehicles, etc, can all be deadly to the time traveler.

Let's go 1000 years in the future once again and take our time machine out in the desert to test it. We set the clock to May 12, 1950, and go back in time. As we materialize, we find that we are in a top secret testing zone for a nuclear weapon, seconds before it detonates. Unfortunately, we, and our machine, are destroyed, so no other experiments are attempted because we never returned to tell of our success. If nothing else, we might have the misfortune of materializing in the middle of a tree that died years ago or on top of a cow that happened to be passing by. Any obstacle, either stationary or moving, could be disastrous. On the other hand, certain landmarks could be good, even invaluable. The hangar is just that. A permanent landmark, always cared for and, hopefully, clear of obstacles.

7/17/99

I didn't sleep very well last night. I had a lot of weird dreams that kept waking me up. Right now I couldn't tell you what any of them were about. So, if my writing is sloppy, it's because I'm tired.

Presently I'm at Griffith Park. I drove over here so I could get away and write some. It's more peaceful than the apartment.

Let me continue with my explanation.

One day I was sitting in my car on lunch-break from work when the idea came to me how I could bypass the enormity of the hangar experiment. I needed a way to conduct the experiment on my own. The idea culminated in the form of this notebook.

The journal is better than the hangar idea because it doesn't worry about how time travel happens, it just requires contact from a future traveler. This book is a map, a record, an itinerary of times and places that can be followed.

There are unfortunately still a few variables, which if not fulfilled, will leave the book impotent.

    # 1. Ability of time travel.
        If time travel is never achieved, then there will be no contact.

    # 2. Time travelers wanting to contact me.
        Why would they want to contact me? Wouldn't Einstein or Steven Hawking be better?

    # 3. Book is renowned in the future.
        The purpose of the book is to somehow make it to the future for this to work. My experiment either has to be known to the masses or just to those who have the time machines.

Think about time being fluid, flexible. Consider this—while you are reading this sentence, I am somewhere else in time writing it out, right now. Strange idea sure, but that's just the beginning of the conundrums. You could even say that you are reading this sentence at one point in time and there's another point in time where I haven't even written it down yet.

If you think about time as a movie shown from a film projector, and you are watching the movie, then you only see what's before your eyes on the screen. If you're half-way through the movie, then you know all the characters' names and the plot that's going on, but you don't know the ending. Yet the ending is lying on the film reel, it just hasn't reached your eyes yet. As well, the beginning of the movie is still there too, but it has already past your line of sight and gone on. The film still exists in its entirety, but your perception tells you that one portion is gone and the other is yet to come.

With that in mind, here's my next paradox. Anyone reading this journal in the future could influence the success of my experiment by doing something very strange. After reading it, wrap it up in an air tight, waterproof container. Then take it out somewhere and bury it in the ground. Be sure to write your name in it so the future can give you credit when they find it. Someone might discover it while digging up what used to be your backyard to build a skyscraper, or maybe during an archeological excavation. If you're reading this then that means my book is finished to some degree, and the fact that you decide to bury it can affect the success of my writing it now. Once the book is found by someone in the future, then the future can contact me, and that, in return, affects me here as I'm writing.

That is what this notebook is all about. The journal entries will be recording my times, logging dates and places, and telling of any experiences that occur. This way, if time travel becomes possible, then finding me will be a matter of having this book. Of course my book, like the hangar, has to stand the test of time for this to work. If I'm not contacted, then it may mean no one ever found out about my book, or possibly that time travel never happened.

I can already see that there will be setbacks, like busy schedules, that will give gaps in the journal entry dates. But I'm also planning ahead, hopefully, that the integrity of the journal will be kept through the editing process so that no discrepancies will occur for future references. Hopefully, my friend Calvin will agree to do any editing necessary. He's always been my creative partner, and a pretty resourceful person, too.

7/17/99

After that last entry, I drove back to my apartment to look up some things.

Thinking about books making their way through time, I started re-reading some of Shakespeare's sonnets, and two in particular stuck out. From Shakespeare's writings it seems like he knew, or maybe he just hoped, that his work would survive the centuries. Some of the sonnets hint that future generations will be reading his writings. One example is sonnet #55, which begins with the lines:

> Not marble, nor the gilded monuments
> Of princes, shall outlive this powerful rime;

Translated, it means marble structures and gold-covered statues of dead princes will fade away and rust, but my poetry will last longer than any of them.

Another example of Shakespeare's knowledge of future readers is the end of sonnet #18, which says;

> So long as men can breath, or eyes can see
> So long lives this and this gives life to thee.

Shakespeare, almost 400 years ago, had the audacity to think that today we would still be reading and talking about his writings, and we are.

It may be easy to misconstrue Shakespeare as being vain because of his belief in his lasting works, but it wasn't vanity that he displayed, it was hope. He never knew what would happen to his legacy, at least we don't think he knew. But he wrote as if he were hoping for the future. If at times my writings seem vain, trust me they're not, it's just positive and hopeful thinking.

7/18/99

There was a young lady named Bright,
Whose speed was far faster than light.
She went out one day,
In a relative way,
And returned the previous night!
                    -Reginald Buller

Tomorrow I have to go back to work, so hopefully I can finish explaining this project before the end of the day today.

Projecting images to the past is one theory that I think holds the strongest possibility for time experiments. Another one consists of viewing the past but not traveling there.

The idea that one day we'll be able to project an image to the past isn't too far off. In order to do this, you will need to either accelerate light past it's own speed or discover what scientists call a tachyon. Tachyons are hypothetical particles that travel faster than the speed of light. According to relativity, anything traveling faster than the speed of light would go backward in time. Because of light's simplicity, it would be easier to transport than a human's body.

If you could make a projector that shot tachyon rays and projected it on the wall inside a house, then the image would appear in the past instead of the present. Someone standing in front of the wall five minutes ago, or five years ago, might see the image. The distance the image would travel backward in time would depend on the speed of the tachyon beam. A symbol projected on the wall, hanging in mid air, or anywhere, could be the first or only form of contact to be made.

I want to describe my second theory as thoroughly as possible, but it involves a little lesson in film. The trick to getting a picture to appear as though it's moving on a screen is very interesting. What most people should know, if they don't, is that motion pictures are just a succession of still photos shown at a rate of 24 frames per second. Few would argue that movies are illusions, but the idea of a "motion picture" is an illusion in itself. The term used to describe this phenomenon of motion is "Persistence of vision." Getting a bunch of pictures to look like a single moving picture is all a trick.

Still photography works differently from film in many aspects. One main difference is the way you light your subject. Since a still photo takes only a fraction of a second to accomplish the task, you only need a fraction of a second of light. Like the flash on any 35mm camera, it lights up your subject for a portion of a second. The big boys though, the ones who shoot supermodels for the front of *Vogue* magazine, use large "power packs" to power their flashes. These are usually referred to as "strobes."

There is a strange effect that happens when you use a strobe light on a spinning fan, like a ceiling fan or floor fan. And, for this, I don't mean just a quick pop of the strobe but instead you need a strobe that continuously flashes. When the frequency of the strobe light is slower than the fan, the fan will appear as though it is moving slower than normal. As you increase the frequency of the strobe, the fan appears to move slower and slower, until you reach a point when the fan appears to stop spinning The fan and the strobe have reached the same frequency when this happens. At this point, if you continue to gradually increase the frequency of the strobe, it will appear as though the fan is moving backwards. The more the strobe frequency is turned up, the faster backwards the fan seems to turn, until it stops again. This, of course, is an optical illusion and the fan is still moving at the same rate the entire time, but visually it is stopping and then moving backwards.

Here's another interesting thing about vision and the brain. There was a film I remember seeing in psychology class that showed a woman who had brain damage from a disease or severe flu. Her brain damage wasn't normal, though (if you consider any damage normal). The problem was that her thinking skills were all intact and she talked quite coherently, but one part of her brain in particular was affected. She saw everything, not in motion, but in a series of still pictures. Every few seconds she would see a picture of her surroundings and that image would hold in her brain until the next one would come and replace it.

They gave examples of how she had to be careful not to overfill a glass of water as she poured it, because she saw the glass empty, and the next picture she saw, it was running over. The scariest example was of her trying to cross the street. You can probably imagine the difficulty of crossing the street when all you see is a staccato of cars coming around the corner and a "walk" sign that may not say "walk" anymore.

It would appear that not only does light have a pulse and show motion, but also our brain has a sensor for motion. If that sensor is shut off or disturbed, then still pictures are all we see. What if life has a pulse, a frequency even? And if you find it and change its rhythm then you can change the way we see time. Not that you could go back or forth in time, but just look backward or forward, and more than likely just backward. This is purely hypothetical, but if you had such a device then you could set it up anywhere you wanted and turn the frequency back until you saw people walking around that had been there hours ago. Turn it up further and see days, maybe even years in the past. The people wouldn't really be there, of course, it would just be their images.

This idea isn't that far off when you think of infrared and heat sensors that exist today. With heat sensing devices, you can see people's images seconds after they have left a room because of the heat trail they leave behind.

There is a theory called "String Theory," which postulates that subatomic particles are made up of tiny vibrating "strings." These "strings" are supposedly all the same, but the different vibrations determine the function of the particle. One type of vibration could make the particle a quark, and another vibration could make it an electron. It all depends on the frequency. There is also the idea that, within this theory of vibrating strings there are several dimensions, not just the "commonly known" three dimensions. This is where my theory of a pulse within nature shows similarities. If you change this pulse or vibration of the string, could you manipulate dimensions? Maybe even speed up or slow down the atoms? If you could change the frequency of the subatomic particles, then maybe you could manipulate nature, or even time, much like the fan and the strobe light.

9:08 PM 7/19/99

I don't know if I can do this. This book may prove impossible for me to write. At work today, I started wondering if someone around me was a covert spy, wearing clothes and mimicking behavior that fit this time period but secretly sent back in time to observe me. Then I started seeing them all over the place, following me, looking me in the eyes. No one in California looks you in the eyes. They were walking close to me in the grocery store, walking up behind me to see what I was getting at the seafood counter, then as I walked away telling the butcher that they were "just looking." You see how this could drive a person to paranoia? I'm not sure I want to put myself through this.

I'm sitting here in my apartment, and I've just pulled out my College Psychology book and looked up paranoid schizophrenia. It says: "Prominent features are delusions of persecution or grandeur accompanied by anger, superiority, argumentativeness, etc. Paranoid schizophrenia tends to appear later in life, typically after the age of twenty five or thirty."

I just turned twenty-five last month! That's starting to hit a little too close to home. A person could easily drive himself insane by keeping up an idea like this for very long. And where would it end? If this experiment reaches publication (or even becomes a complete book), do I walk around the rest of my life with these delusional ideas popping in and out of my head? I'll have to give this some serious thought.

This is a tricky dilemma. Do I stop writing and save my sanity or keep looking for signs of contact and possibly lose my mind?

7/20/99 11:26 AM
I feel a lot better today. I'm not feeling as paranoid, but I'm becoming more concerned about the book's future. Will it be a piece of literature that people know about twenty years from now, or will it be lost in my attic and discovered by my grandchildren? The latter is more likely, and my grandchildren will think I'm a crazy old man.

I noticed earlier that I started my first entry with the wrong month. I put 6/15/99 instead of 7/15/99. I've corrected it now, but that could be a costly mistake for what I'm trying to do. From now on, for the purity of the journal, I can't allow myself to go back and change anything else on previous pages. I can only mention it later. I'll just have to double-check my dates for accuracy.

7/20/99 5:00 PM
As the day progresses, a few perplexing ideas have surfaced. First, I'm wondering what kind of a paper trail I'm leaving behind (besides my journal) that is accurate and traceable.

I just returned from the gas station, where I used a credit card at the pump. Somewhere there is a computer system that records my name, exact time, and place where I bought gas. Next I went to the store and made a purchase at the pharmacy using my ATM card. There are at least two traces left behind, one on the computer and another on my bank records, which leave both a paper and digital trail. Then I came home and wrote down the transaction in my checkbook, which gives another record, and I also filed the receipt in my file folder.

I'm trying to think of all the ways to track a person back in time from the future, even track them to specific times and locations. Not that my file cabinet records will last a thousand years, but no one can be sure how soon time travel technology will come about or how long computer records will be around.

7/20/99 8:23 PM
On my way downstairs to get the mail a few minutes ago, I thought of another problem. What if I was contacted through a letter in the mail? Would I report something like that in my journal? I know what you're

thinking. One of my friends could drop me a letter as a joke. No, no one knows about this experiment except for me. And I won't tell anyone about it until it's finished. But my point is that if future generations see that I'm ready and willing, even waiting, to write down evidence of time travel, they might decide not to contact me. With "The Hangar Theory" it was to be kept a secret and away from the public. What would writing down a contact from the future do?

Then I came up with an idea. What if I was to write down a word here in the journal, some word that's not used very often, and made this my signal? Now this would reverse the rules of contact. Instead of them being the sender and I the receiver, I would be giving them a signal to send back to me. That might be a way to contact me without as much risk. Maybe "Harmonica" would be a good word to use. So if I'm walking to my car in the morning and find a piece of paper on the ground with "Harmonica" written on it, or see it written in graffiti as I'm driving to work, then this could be a strange, but positive, signal. Now that I've written the word down in my journal for the future to know, it should open up the possibilities of me seeing or hearing the word.

What if a word isn't good? What if a picture worked better, and a simple picture at that? Something they could project back in time. If so, then giving the future a drawing might be a good idea.

This is a good, simple drawing, yet different enough not to be a frequent symbol in everyday life.

7/21/99
Today I was not thinking much at all about the "harmonica" word or the drawing. Work was too crazy to think about much else.

There's this older guy I work with named Allen who is Hispanic. From what he says, his mother didn't want him to have a Mexican name. (I say Hispanic but he wants to be called Mexican, he hates the politically correct thing). Out of everyone who sells cameras at my job, he's the only one I care to talk to. Anyway, he had the flu last week and just came back to work today. He still sounds pretty bad, and today one of these "professional" photographers came in and wanted Allen to demonstrate how to use a certain type camera, and Allen obliged. The "professional" photographer didn't even know how to turn on the camera. Allen showed him how to do it and after showing him where the "on" button was for the third time, Allen started coughing really bad. This photographer guy thought Allen was trying to avoid talking to him and picked up the camera and threw it over the counter at Allen. Luckily it missed hitting him.

Anyway, this customer must be a big shot or something because he went and complained to the manager, and the manager ended up reprimanding Allen for not being more patient with the customer.

Just thought I would give an example of what it's like in Los Angeles at this point in time, and especially in this business.

7/23/99

Why would someone from the future want to contact me anyway?
Some odd man in the past that happened to write a strange little book.
And if my theory is right about the government or military being the
ones to discover the capabilities and create the apparatus, then why
would they care about contacting me?

Oh, here's a twist I just thought about. Let's say even further into the
future, say 100 years after the government has created the time
machine, there are the equivalent of today's computer hackers.
Renegades who created their own machines, or find a way to get into
the government's machine and attempt to contact me. That could be
possible. Or here's another idea: what if after the machine's creation
the government is taken over by "the people" or even another
government. Maybe they would use it.

Then that brings up the question of whether to trust any contact to be
friendly. What would anyone's reason be for coming to see me?
Should I assume they would be friendly? What would their
motivations be?

7/24/99

For some reason I feel it's best not to give out the name of my employer or the apartment where I live. I just feel apprehensive about it. There's no reason to give out that information. Besides, I have a couple of roommates I live with, and I don't want anyone, except me, involved in this. One of my roommates is my girlfriend, Surrey. We met about two-and-a-half years ago. She says she moved from Wyoming to California to be famous. She has no plans on how to do it, she just wants to be famous. Her father would tell you Surrey was named after some place in Canada, but her mom will say it's because they saw the musical *Oklahoma* while she was pregnant with Surrey. My other roommate, Mat, is a guy I met about six months after I moved to California, and we became friends.

I'm all by myself here tonight, though. A couple of our friends wanted to go out clubbing and running around. Mat and Surrey went, but I decided to stay home. I'm not really into that kind of thing. Besides, it's easier to think and write when people aren't here.

I just finished watching a TV program about films, computers, technologies, and how they're all advancing at such a rapid pace. Computers are doubling in speed every couple of years, a genetic map is being created that could cure all human diseases, and now cloning could become a common practice in the near future. Advancements in the sciences are happening at such a stunning rate that I could see time manipulations within one hundred years. Of course I could just be riding on the hype of the TV program, but the advances truly are compounding at an enormous rate.

7/27/99

An epiphany of sorts struck me tonight about this book. Let's imagine that this book makes its way into mainstream society, and becomes canonized literature when time manipulation is possible. Now if the book is widely accepted, or at least accepted by those who control the time machine, then I may be contacted or I may not, just that simple. Right?

Now let's look at it from a different angle. Let's use the process of elimination. If the book is looked down on in the future, despised, or causes chaos for those who control time manipulation, then my guess is that I would have been contacted by them already, and in a way that wouldn't be healthy for me.

So, I can't say anything about the future except this: if time manipulation becomes possible and my book becomes known, then it will be well-accepted or at least tolerated, but definitely not disruptive. If it were disruptive then they would have already taken me out, like the Mafia does.

7/28/99

I might as well start occasionally listing where I am in order to either prove or rule out the possibility of being contacted.

It is 6:00 PM and I am stopped at Carl's Jr. on Hollywood Way and Verdugo in Burbank CA. to pick up a hamburger. That's interesting. As soon as I finished writing that last sentence, a man parked beside me in a brand new white Ford Explorer. He was watching me write in my notebook, before he got out of his car. That brings up an even more perplexing issue that I was trying to avoid. With the story of "The Hangar Theory" when the hangar door is closed the likelihood of someone appearing immediately is just as strong as the likelihood of an appearance 10 years later. What I'm saying is that, as soon as I wrote down the location and the time, 6:00 PM 7/28/99, just like the plaque on the wall in the story, the likelihood of someone showing up here was very strong. That's why I was so intrigued just now by the gentleman that pulled up beside me when I finished that sentence. It was like closing the hangar door. Was he a contact? I don't know.

8/03/99

Here's a clue that time is passing by, I was getting ready for work this morning and I just so happened to find a gray hair on my head, and this is a first for me. I kept looking and found a couple more hidden in what used to be solid brown hair. Sure it sounds very petty, and I probably shouldn't be writing about it, but it does have to do with time and its seemingly inescapable grasp. In my family, I'm the only dark-headed person. That doesn't mean much since I'm the only child. But my dad's hair is sandy blonde and my mom's was too. My mom passed away in June of 1996.

So, I'm starting to envy the blonde thing because you can't really tell the white hairs from the gray. It goes without saying that I pulled the gray hair out and hoped, in vain, not to get any more. Soon there'll be more, but I won't start coloring my hair as I get older. I like the idea of aging naturally, just not this early.

What causes our bodies to age? How does everything in life know and feel the effects of time? Is there anything that escapes its laws?

I guess I made this entry just to complain about time.

8/04/99

I guess I started something yesterday that I should explain.

My mom had a heart condition from birth. She knew about the condition since she was about ten years old. My dad and I had gone with her to interview several specialists leading up to 1996, but there wasn't much that could be done. After several years of researching we found that surgery was more risky than just living with the condition. Anyway, one day she was in a department store and told a salesperson that she had to lie down. She never got up again.

I didn't want to put a depressing mood over the journal but, since I mentioned it yesterday, I felt that an explanation was necessary. And one thing I can't do is go back and add or erase anything that I've already written. That is one of the rules to writing this journal.

8/10/99

Once again I am wondering why anyone would contact me unless I had something to offer. Maybe offering anonymity is enough. Maybe they wouldn't be able to contact me until the book is finished, to ensure that the book is completed. They might be afraid that their presence in a different time would get recorded in my journal. Maybe the renegades will be the initiators and won't want to risk being found out.

8/11/99

I'm going to try something new. The time is 5:41 PM, and I am stopped at a red light on my way home from work listening to 91.5 FM, which is a classical music radio station. It hadn't occurred to me to think of the radio as a means of communication but maybe a piece of music will play over the air that will give me a clue. A blues station might work better than a classical station, just so I can listen for a harmonica tune. It's very difficult to write and drive simultaneously, especially with a manual transmission, and (illegible phrase), but I hate pulling over. Seems like when you really need a red light you can't catch one to save your life. I've gone through several green lights now that any other day would inevitably be red.

8/11/99

Well I'm home now and the time is 5:57 PM. Maybe it's a good thing I didn't hear any voices through the radio, but they are playing some really good music. Later on I'll call the station and ask them to look up the classical piece they played and I'll write down what it was.

8/13/99

I called KUSC radio station after arriving home and asked for their music library, which is a wonderful service. Giving them the time span I was listening to their station, they gave me the piece that was being played during that interim. The Moldau, by Bedrich Smetana, is what the gentleman said I heard that evening. Considering there might be a clue in the music, I wrote down the name. I plan on buying the music at some point in the future.

Most of the time while making journal entries or anticipating contacts, I'm looking less for a direct contact and more for just observers (people watching me or acting peculiar, something out of the ordinary).

But a contact might not happen even if all the variables take place, since any direct contact might jeopardize the book. This assumes the book takes hold and means something relevant to the future. If so, then contact may only happen, if ever, after the book is finished so that the book completes its journey through time. This brings me back to people observing. They shouldn't have any effect if they are only watching me, right?

8/15/99

I've probably been reading too much Einstein or thinking too much about time travel for my own good. Last night I had a bad dream.

I was in my hometown of Austin, and I was walking down the street next to the Capitol building. Everything was very detailed in the dream and extremely vivid.

As I walked up to the Capitol building, I noticed it was beautifully set in front of an ocean-blue sky. The wind was blowing slightly and the air had a humid warmth to it. There was this bronze plaque erected out on the front of the lawn with raised lettering on it, like most historical markers that you see. Thinking it had something to do with the building, I walked up to read it. A quick look and I knew the writing was not in English, and it wasn't any language that I could recognize. I ran my hands over the letters for some reason, thinking maybe it would help, and then I noticed a raised circular button in the middle. It didn't appear to be a part of the writing. But for some reason, in that dream-world haze, I realized it was the button I was looking for, so I pushed it. Then the small bronze button began moving downward into the plaque very slowly. Once it became flush with the rest of the plaque, it stopped. The wind started blowing and the sky started forming a bubble on the horizon, as if the earth's atmosphere was closing in on me.

As it made it's way toward me, I could see the trees and buildings aging. Everywhere I looked, the land beyond the bubble was old, gray, and decayed. As the anomaly reached the Capitol Building, I thought it would kill me, but instead it surrounded me. The wind died down and the beautiful blue aura stopped, in an egg-like shape, around me. Then I realized that my family lived in this town. What had become of them? Did I cause this to happen?

I felt something rub against my leg. I looked down and noticed a cat winding around my feet. I hadn't noticed it there before. The cat looked up at me and then walked toward the edge of the blue bubble. Suddenly, I realized what would happen if the cat passed through the shell, so I reached down to stop the cat, but it was too late. What happened to the cat was so shocking that it woke me up.

As I sat in bed I felt very vulnerable. For the rest of the day I couldn't shake that feeling. And even now, some fifteen hours later, as I lay in bed again writing about it, I'm wondering if I should call home. Have you ever had one of those dreams, one that affects the entire day?

8/18/99

There have been a lot of thoughts running through my head that I haven't had time to write down. Most of them I manage to jot down on a piece of paper or remember for later, but I must confess some of them slip by me. Reading back through my notes, I've come up with a few ideas that I'll attempt to tie together in a relevant way. If I stray or ramble, forgive me.

My thoughts keep returning to the idea of a time line. The theory of a time line, as I perceive it, is this: for time travel to be possible, time has to be constant, not only happening now, but also in the past and future at the same time. All three, past, present, and future, have to be happening now, and always happening continuously, at every point in time. Let me give an example:

This line represents time, which we will begin at Shakespeare's birth in 1564, and continue to an arbitrary point in the future like 2090 A.D. Now if the time line idea is true, then any and every point on the line between 1564 A.D. and 2090 A.D. is happening right now and will always be happening just like a moving assembly line. If you look at any point on a conveyer belt of an assembly line, you will see the product in motion, and yet constantly showing the same thing being repeated, always replenishing, always happening. The product at the beginning of the conveyer belt is just falling on while the one at the end is just falling off, which keeps the flow of product, in our case the product is time, continually coming and going.

If the time line idea is not true, then time travel may not be possible. How else would you be able to travel there if it were not still happening? I could be flawed in my ideas, but wouldn't it be just like normal travel? You can't drive some place that isn't there, and you can't go back to Shakespeare's time if it's not happening right now at a different point in time.

Now take the 7/28/99 entry at the Carl's Jr. restaurant. If the time line theory is correct, and time manipulation is happening right now at some point in time, then the future and I may be influencing one another, even communicating to each other.

Let's say the future is reading this book right now and they read the entry 7/28/99 and there wasn't any mention of a man in a white Ford Explorer. They make a decision to send a man back with clothes and money to purchase whatever he needs. Then they tell him to be at Carl's Jr. on the date in the journal, but just to observe. He buys a white Ford Explorer and arrives at the location and observes. When I see him I log it in my book. That immediately changes the journal. After I make my entry, the future knows that he made it, either intentionally or by a foul up on their part, because his sighting is now listed in the journal, whereas it wasn't before. Only one problem arises here though, if I can have an effect on them, and communicate with the future, then that means time is able to change.

Reading over the above paragraph, after a 30-minute break, I can see holes in the idea. Basically, if the timeline theory is true and everything is happening now, present as well as future, then couldn't I influence them as much as they could me?

8/19/99

It's lunchtime for me at work, and a late one at that. The camera store I work at is here in Hollywood, a few blocks up from Wilshire Boulevard. My lunch hours are never the same, sometimes lunch is at noon and other times at 4:00 PM, it all depends on what time your shift started. I like working with cameras, but this job is really getting to me. That's one reason I take my lunch breaks here in the car rather than in the lunchroom with the others. It's my escape.

Anyway, I thought that lunch breaks in my car might be a good time to start writing journal entries. The streets here are very pretty and the houses are fairly expensive older homes. Some of them have a stucco look, or an adobe finish, and others are just brick. The neighborhood has beautiful large trees lining the streets. And when the leaves start falling here in a couple of months, the streets will fill with huge brown leaves, and they'll blow down the street and make a wonderful, quiet, rustling sound. What better place than this to sit and write?

So I just finished my sandwich, and the time is 4:45 PM, and I am in my Jeep on the corner of Orange Dr. and 2nd Street in Hollywood, CA. As I finished that last sentence, I took a couple of minutes to look around for suspicious people walking or driving by, but saw no one. Now it is 4:51 PM according to the car clock.

I would like to add something to yesterday's writing while I'm thinking about it. Sitting here looking at this nice neighborhood, the thought just occurred to me that there's no reason for time travelers to be limited to my entry dates to contact me, they could arrive before I write down my location. They could have started renting a house here along the street in anticipation of this entry in order to watch me from their window. Nothing says they can't arrive early for a good seat.

But this brings up another variable, the dependency of my writing down the entry. In my time, right here and now, nothing is guaranteed until it happens. I could have planned on writing this journal entry 20 minutes ago but been killed somehow, or the journal could have been destroyed in a fire, and planning to make a journal entry would have stayed just that, a plan. But once I actually made the entry it was finalized in this time. Take the hangar theory again, the future time travelers could have shown up a year before the plaque date, but that would have jeopardized the hangar being completed. The same goes for this journal. If a contact interferes with me before the entry, then they might jeopardize the book being completed. Then, if the book isn't completed, they have no reference to come back to. This is starting to become confusing.

8/20/99

I hate to keep contradicting myself, but maybe I was wrong yesterday. Maybe everything is guaranteed and unchangeable. If everything happens past, present, and future simultaneously, then the first appearance by time travelers in the hangar happened at the same time that the machine was built, and yet before it was built. The same applies with the man in the white Ford Explorer. If he was from the future, then he arrived, I wrote down his arrival, and the people building the machine read about it, all at the same time. Now how does that happen?

I know I'm not coming up with any clear-cut answers, but I didn't expect to figure it all out anyway.

All of this reminds me of the book of Revelation in the Bible. If the book is true, then how could God tell us about the future, and we see it happening, and it still happen? Some might say it's self-fulfilling prophecy, but then that would be even stranger, to make the future happen by telling how it's going to happen. It's like the scene in the movie "The Matrix" where Reeves' character goes to see the Oracle and she says to him, "don't worry about the vase" and he replies, "what vase?" then turns around and knocks the vase off the table and breaks it. He wouldn't have knocked it off if she hadn't said anything, would he? Is that self-fulfilling prophecy? Does this idea prove what I said earlier that everything is guaranteed, meaning unchangeable? If so, then God telling us about the future in Revelation wouldn't change it. It has already happened in the future. That's how God could say it and not jeopardize the outcome.

It's like taking an imaginary wind-up clock and winding the hour hand from 11:00 AM backwards to 9:00 AM and then letting it go. The clock runs forward but it knows where it will end up as well as all the points in between, because it's already been there.

8/24/99

Today Allen and I went to lunch together at Pink's off La Brea Blvd. I was surprised because we rarely have our lunch breaks scheduled together. It was nice, though. We sat and ate hot dogs and talked.

I told Allen I wasn't so sure I was supposed to be out here in California. Allen told me his parents both moved from El Paso to California because they had relatives that lived out here. His parents got married in Chihuahua, Mexico, and became nationalized U.S. citizens shortly thereafter. Allen grew up in East Los Angeles but lives in Hollywood now. We started talking about fate and destiny, and he said that he believes in fate very much, and that fate brought him to live in Hollywood and to work with cameras.

I told him I believed in the Heavenly Muses but wasn't so sure about the Fates. He said when he was growing up, he didn't believe in them either, but one day his dog ran away and he started trusting the Fates. I thought he was making a joke, so I started laughing. But then he began telling me the story.

When he was a teenager, he had this German Shepherd named Rascal that he'd raised from a puppy. The dog would occasionally get in trouble, but wasn't as bad as the other dogs in the neighborhood. Allen would let the dog sleep with him in his bed, and he made sure to play with the dog and take him for plenty of walks and stuff. Well, one day Allen was out walking Rascal in a different neighborhood, when he heard a dog barking ferociously from behind a fence in a back yard. No sooner had Allen turned and looked, when he saw a Pit Bull jump the fence and start running after them. As Allen took off running, he heard the guy who owned the Pit Bull come out of his front door, calling for the dog to stop. The next thing he heard was a horrible dog fight happening, and when he turned around he saw that Rascal hadn't run away and was tearing into the Pit Bull as best as possible. The other dog's owner was trying to pull the Pit Bull away, but got bitten in the process. So Allen ran back to the dogs and tried to do something, but all he could do was scream and wait for the dogs to stop.

Eventually, the dogs got tired and stopped. Allen could see that the Pit Bull had Rascal by the neck. The other dog's owner wrapped a collar around the Pit Bull and kicked him in the ribs 'til he let go. By that time Rascal had lost some blood.

The guy that owned the Pit Bull locked his dog in the house and loaded Rascal into his truck. They drove to the nearest veterinary and had Rascal treated. The other guy paid for everything, probably because he didn't want his dog taken away or have charges pressed.

Anyway, Allen took Rascal home all bandaged up, and it took awhile for the dog to heal. Allen made sure to take good care of the dog the entire time. But the day that the bandages came off for good Rascal ran away from home. Allen looked in all the familiar places, including the parks they visited, but didn't find Rascal anywhere. A couple of weeks went by, and Allen's father told him to give up, that finding Rascal alive at this point was probably impossible. A couple of days later, Allen's uncle came to visit and was asking him about the dog. When Allen told him the story, his uncle said, "let the Fates guide you." Allen didn't know what Fates were (he wasn't even much of a Catholic). But as his uncle began telling him about it, Allen started to feel something good come over him. He found that he was trusting in something that he couldn't explain. But apparently, Allen's father was upset that his uncle had given him hope in such a grim situation. But with a newfound confidence, Allen headed out again. He went only in the directions that felt good to him and ended up a couple of miles from home.

He started doubting himself and the Fates when he came to a dead end street as the sun was going down. He turned around a couple of times and finally walked toward a house that had some blue trim around the bottom. As he approached, he saw a rectangular hole in the wood that was used for a crawl space under the house. He put his head through the hole and saw his dog sitting there with five little puppies nursing from her.

He found out later that the owner of the house didn't know whose dog it was but had been taking care of her and giving her food and water.

So he left the dog there a couple more weeks to let the pups get strong enough so he could take them home. Apparently, a few months earlier, Allen had awakened to find a neighbor dog in his backyard playing with Rascal. He took the male mutt back to the neighbor but didn't even think about them making puppies.

Honestly, I wasn't really sure if Allen was telling me the truth or not. So, on the way back to work, I ask him if the story was real. He showed me a picture he had in his wallet of a dog that he said was the great grandpuppy of Rascal.

We were about twenty minutes late getting back to the camera store and the manager was upset. He had mistakenly scheduled us together for lunch and said it wouldn't happen again.

8/25/99

Lunch time again, and I'm at the corner of Orange Dr. and 2nd street in Hollywood. The time is 1:10 PM, and I would like to propose a dare to the future. Maybe contact won't work because it would mess things up, but I would just like to see a confirmation. A woman with dark hair and wearing a black dress could pull up across the street from my blue Jeep and get out, then walk to a house across the street, that would be all I ask for.

It's 1:15 PM, now. Well, that was exciting. At 1:12 PM about a block away from me a woman pulled up, got out and walked across to a house on my side of the street, but she had auburn hair and wore a gray suit. She waved at someone in the house as she walked across the street. I was excited for a minute. That was a pretty strange coincidence, the best thing that's happened with the experiment so far.

8/25/99

It's 5:05 PM now and I just got off work. Assuming that incident earlier was real, maybe the woman crossing the street was just a test. They wanted to see if I would write down the occurrence, and if I hadn't, they might have trusted me with something bigger next time. In the future I might discriminate on what is entered in the journal. Show them that I'm trustworthy.

8/26/99

With my luck, if this journal is studied at all in the future it won't be in the science classes. Instead, they'll deconstruct me in the psychology classes. "Scholars, this is Psychosis in its rawest documented form."

Often I see people, complete strangers, looking at me as if they recognize me. I know I don't look like anyone famous, so I entertain the idea that it has to do with my journal. And, of course, I wouldn't dream of walking up to any of these people and saying anything. That would surely land me in the loony bin. Even if someone came up to me, talking about the future and time travel, unprompted, I would probably question their sanity. And I'm actually looking for a contact like that!

8/27/99

I haven't forgotten or given up on my word and symbol from the journal entry. What I need to do is start finding a wider variety of locations to experiment with. Looking back at "The Hangar Theory" I see the need for a sturdy, appropriate environment to go back to, one that won't change too much over time.

Let's say, just for laughs, that California does fall into the ocean. Then the location of Orange Dr. and 2nd street, that I've previously listed, won't exist in the future. In my theory, if the hangar had been blown away by a tornado or collapsed in an earthquake 50 years before the time machine was built, then there wouldn't be a place to travel back from, no place of origin. That's one reason I want to start listing various locations in my journal, to give more chances for the future to play with. Just in case some environments are more stable than others.

And, in case the future wants to leave me a message, I have a voice mail number. They can call and just say "harmonica" if they want. The number is 818-----------. The number isn't doing me any good, and I've only paid for about six more months of use. I just hope I can publish the phone number without any trouble.

8/31/99

If you could go back to the past and change one part of your life, would you really do it? Is there something that pervades your everyday life so much that you feel you'd be better off if it hadn't happened?

It's a hard decision, but I think I've come up with one. You'd probably guess that I'd go back and tell my mom to be careful with her heart condition, but that wouldn't help. It was a congenital problem. She had known about it for a long time, and there was really nothing that could have been done differently. Of course, I would love to see her again, but it might just make things even harder.

What I'd do is pick something that could be changed. Mine goes back to when I was in junior high. There was this ring that I had, which my grandfather had given to me. It was a gold ring with a couple of small diamonds set inside a flat surface. It wasn't anything amazing, but it was old and it had come from my grandfather before he died. I was particularly enamored with it because it was so old and, even though it was too big for my finger, I wore it all the time. My dad said that he even remembered the ring from when he was a child. He reminded me how precious it was, and that I had to be responsible for taking care of the ring.

One day, my friend came over and asked if I wanted to go swimming in a nearby creek. So I put on my shorts and we went hiking. We walked through our neighbor's pasture and down the hill to the only swimming place within miles. We had swimming contests and played tag, and before we knew it it was getting time to go home. When I got out of the water, I noticed that the ring was gone. I realized it must be somewhere in that muddy, clay-colored water that we'd been playing in. There was no chance of finding it, I knew that, but I started to dive for it anyway, just in case. My friend helped for a while then gave up and went home. I kept diving over and over again, knowing that my father would find out sooner or later. He wouldn't forgive me either, and I was truly at fault. Before I knew it, the sun was going down, and I looked up and saw two girls sitting on the opposite bank watching me. I couldn't hear them, but I was sure they were laughing at me. A couple more dives and finally I gave up. My heart sank because I loved that ring as much as my father did, but I had been careless with it just as he presumed I would be. I wanted to just sit there on the bank of the creek and never leave, but I had to go home.

When my father came home from work I told him right away what had happened. He didn't say a thing. My parents grounded me for two weeks, and if that had been the end of it I would have been happy. But it was my first experience with a true feeling of total loss. The aching bitterness of my own actions hung over me and wouldn't let go. I couldn't get over how careless I had been.

My father couldn't bring himself to talk to me for several days, and, after that, I noticed a change in his mood when anything went wrong. It seemed my dad would blame me when something came up broken or missing. He had no idea that I was still beating myself up, and that his actions just compounded the effect. Before this, I don't think I knew what insecurity felt like. But now I couldn't escape it.

But I was young, and maybe I'm putting too much into this. And some people would probably say that it's all a part of growing up, and losing one's innocence.

I just don't know. I don't tend to get along with my dad now, especially with mom gone. There seems to be a distance there. We talk, but it isn't like it used to be. I guess I could just bring it up next time I'm home. Clear the air.

9/2/99

Maybe the timeline theory is wrong and "now" only comes once. No second chances for anything. Once a moment has passed, it's gone forever. That theory doesn't appeal to me, though. The timeline idea is still the most fun to play with. The possibilities are enormous. It feels like a chess game, trying to imagine all the moves and counter moves possible between the future and the present.

9/14/99

I wonder what the limits are to my requests, or "dares," in the journal. They have to be reasonable, obviously, something like the woman parking and walking across the street a few weeks ago is good. But what about something a little simpler and more direct?

The time is approximately 3:50 PM, and I am sitting in my blue Jeep on Orange Dr. once again about half a block north of 2nd street. I'll be returning to work at 4:00 PM and leaving at 8:00 PM. A thrilling request to have answered would be to find a note on the windshield of my car when I come back from work. I don't really care what it says, but to have some kind of clue involved would be nice. It sounds silly, but fun.

And since there might be more than one blue Jeep parked here before I return, mine is the one with Texas plates in front of 166 Orange Dr. I know I should have changed to California license plates by now, but please don't tell.

9/14/99 8:24 PM

The time is approximately 8:24 PM. I left work 5 to 10 minutes after 8:00 PM and had forgotten all about the dare until I left work. Work had been too busy to think about it. The walk was about a block and a half, maybe two blocks, to my car, and I wondered if there would be anything on my windshield. As I walked toward my car, a van drove by and blew a ream of paper into the air from the road. I stepped out into the street and saw half a city block, from my Jeep to the end of Orange Dr., littered with paper. The van had run over something, so I went over and found a black attaché case lying in the road. A pen was inside along with a few papers that hadn't blown out.

I went to my car and looked for a note but there wasn't one. But I had a street strewn with papers. Being excited about a correlation, I decided to pick up every paper that was scattered down that street and put them into my car. I drove down to Mansfield Ave., where I parked my Jeep. That is where I am right now sitting and writing.

Looking through the attaché I see a business card with a woman's name on it. The papers appear to be hospital records of this lady, whose name I won't mention. There's a phone number on the card, too. I'm going to call her, of course.

9/17/99

My day was so busy yesterday that I forgot to make an entry to tell about the woman and the notebook. Here's what happened. I returned home excited about the incident and hoping for some kind of clue, so I called her on the phone, but the machine picked up and I left her a message. After waiting a while for a return call I decided to go to the grocery store. When I returned home, my girlfriend, Surrey, told me a woman had called for me. Surrey immediately accused me of cheating, and I spent the next hour trying to explain what happened (without telling her about my book). Surrey eventually left the apartment upset, so I took the opportunity to call the woman about the attaché. She told me she would meet me at my work and pick it up.

I took the attaché with me to work and waited for her. When I returned from lunch an employee told me she had come in looking for me and would return later, but she didn't. The next day she showed up and seemed to be in a hurry. I shook hands with her, gave her the attaché, and she left with a slight "thank you," and nothing else.

Needless to say, I was a little disappointed, not only in the lack of finding a contact, but mostly in the lack of gratitude. She obviously has no idea how far those papers were strewn, or how long it took me to clean them up.

"Plausible Myth," that's what's going through my head right now. It's the only way to describe what I'm doing with this book. This experiment might work, but the chance is so small that I'm better off playing the lottery.

10/01/99 Approximately 8:25 PM

A strange thing happened coming home from work tonight. As I pulled out from my usual parking area at work, heading northbound, I was about to cross the small intersection of 2nd street and Orange Drive. On the other side of the four-way-stop intersection, a man crossed the street carrying a sack of groceries in each hand. He walked painfully slow across the intersection in front of me so I sat at the opposing stop sign waiting for him to cross.

I wasn't in a big hurry, and I didn't want to make the man feel rushed, so I waited. This wasn't an older man, either, only in his late 20's to early 30's. When he reached the other side, he stopped and watched me as I drove by. Then, as I drove off, he continued watching me, just standing there staring at me from the curb. As I watched him in my rear view mirror, a parked car eventually blocked his view of me. That's when he stepped out in the middle of the street and continued to watch me 'til the end of the block. He was still standing there when I reached the next stop sign. I sat there for a moment but eventually had to turn right. That's when I lost sight of him. I wonder if maybe he was an observer who knew of an accident that would happen to me if I hadn't had that moment's delay from him crossing at the intersection. Not a contact, not him violating any interaction law of time travel, just him crossing the street with groceries. That wouldn't get him in trouble, would it?

It was a fun thought, one that stayed with me all the way home. It made me drive a little more cautious too. Maybe that's all the future wants me to do, drive more carefully.

10/11/99 2:43 PM

Here I am on Orange Dr. just south of 2nd street once again. It's
Columbus Day and a lot of people have the day off, but not me. This
whole place is getting to me, both California and this job. I'm so sick
of working here. The drive to work takes me an hour, and I just live 10
miles away. The customers are rude, the pay sucks, the other
employees are either disgruntled or, I don't know what they are, but I
can't stand them. I need a change so bad it hurts, but I'm too afraid.

Anyway, that's not what this entry was supposed to be about. What I
need to do, for the sake of variety, is to start visiting more diverse
places while writing. This whole "Orange Dr. and 2nd street" at
lunchtime is getting old, even though I do enjoy it. Besides the fact that
it's becoming monotonous, there may be better chances to try. Places
like Museums, Libraries, Government buildings, and other structures
that have a good chance of staying around.

Sometimes I wonder if some of these people that live on Orange Dr.
are time travelers set up, before my journal started, to live here and
observe me from their homes. That would be the easiest way, you
know. To travel back means that they wouldn't have to arrive at the
points of entry in my journal. The future could have set up plans long
before I began my journal in expectation of my being on this street. It's
an interesting idea.

For all I know, my entire life could be orchestrated with people from
the future acting as my friends.

10/20/99

Throughout my life, there's been this recurring fantasy that pops in my head about making time stop. It's not the perverted one about going around and taking the clothes off of beautiful women, though every guy has had that fantasy. The fantasy involves stopping time for a duration long enough to catch up on things I would like to have learned. Maybe it's because I didn't take full advantage of my education, but I think it's also from a healthy lust for knowledge. And I'm not fantasizing about stopping time for just minutes or even hours, but years, maybe ten years or more.

In my imaginary world, the present time and place would stop moving forward through time so that nothing would change while I was absent. I would then exist in a type of limbo, and be taken to some place where learning was the only necessity, then later be able to return to the present.

I don't know, maybe it's weird. But I love the idea of being set aside in a different dimension for the sole purpose of learning, with no consequences of time. "Time and Consequences," that sounds like a book title. I'll have to sit down and write that one some day.

11/16/99

I've been so busy lately with work that I haven't been making journal entries as often as I should. The time is 3:30 PM and although I would rather stop making entries while sitting at the intersection of Orange Dr. and 2nd street, it still intrigues me that coincidences happen. I can't decide what to request today so I'll just throw out two random ideas and see if either one materializes.

I would like to make a dare to the future, and it should happen between 3:35 PM and 3:40 PM. If you can produce a blonde man jogging north on Orange Dr. crossing 2nd street in a red running suit, or a small fender bender at the intersection (no one injured), then I think that would be a good sign of confirmation. And I don't want any "almost" or "could be" this time. I don't like having to stretch my imagination to make a connection.

-The time is 3:34 PM now.

-Now it is 3:37 PM according to my car clock.

If my clock is correct, the time is 3:41 PM (which is set for the correct daylight savings time) and no wreck and no blonde jogger in a red suit. A couple of similarities were a blonde boy walking up to the house on the corner with his father. The boy was wearing a red sweatshirt. Then two cars came close to each other at the intersection and one screeched his tires slightly. But the trouble is that I don't want to go for something that isn't obvious. I was reaching for something when those papers were strewn down the city block, and that turned out to be nothing. So let's not reach.

12/01/99

Why are there two men, at least once a week, working on the phone lines on 2nd street? They're doing something with that mainframe box where all those wires run into. That seems a little funny.

One of the dares I would like to try again is the "note on my windshield" dare. Today I get off work at 5:00 PM. The last time I did this, I was excited about picking up half a city block of notebook paper, but I want something real this time. Here goes. The time is 1:54 PM, and my blue Jeep is facing north on Orange Dr. on the east side of the street.

I go back to work from 2:00 PM until 5:00 PM, so we'll see what happens.

12/01/99

Oh yeah! There was a note on my car when I got back from work. It was a parking ticket! As far as I'm concerned this "note on my car" crap is over. I've never been marked or ticketed on Orange Dr. for a parking violation. On other streets, yes, but not this one. And I've been parking here a long time. I don't have the money to pay for this. I'm struggling to pay my bills as it is.

I need to just stop these dares altogether and then throw away this stupid notebook. I'm not getting any results, and for some stupid reason I keep on writing. Unfortunately, this journal has become my only outlet, so I can't just throw it out. But I need to start thinking about when to end this book. I can't keep doing this forever.
By the way, if the future is listening, please have the person fired who gave me the ticket.

12/07/99 8:15 PM
Tonight I am writing from my new apartment, the new apartment
where I now live alone.

You're probably wondering what happened to my girlfriend. Well, I'll
cut to the good part. My "friend" Mat and my "girlfriend" Surrey now
have the apartment together. Yeah, they're still there in the old
apartment, and I found a new place to live. It appears that they had
been enjoying each others' company quite a bit while I wasn't around.

A neighbor in the other apartment complex had asked me one day if
Surrey was sick, because he'd seen her home the day before. I knew
Mat was off that same day; he was off every Thursday. So instead of
asking questions, I decided to investigate. I asked my boss if I could
take off the next Thursday, and I didn't tell Mat or Surrey about it.
That next Thursday I kissed Surrey goodbye in the garage as we both
headed out. I went to a movie and then came back home. Surrey's car
was parked in the driveway and when I went into the apartment they
were there, fully clothed, but cuddled up together on the couch. When I
confronted them, they admitted everything and weren't even upset that
I had caught them. So I packed up and left.

I refrained from writing at the older apartment as much as possible.
Any time I sat down to write in the journal, someone would walk in or
the phone would ring before I could write a full sentence. Instead, I
would go sit by the apartment pool and write, or get by myself on my
day off. Now I have an apartment all of my own, and no one can
disturb me. So I can write all I want.

At times it does get lonely. When you're used to people being around
constantly, it feels strange without them. The longer I'm here, though,
the better it feels. I'll just have to get used to it. The sad thing is that
most of the friends I'd made in the last couple of years were people
Surrey already knew, so they're gone. The only other person I really
talked to was Mat, and now he's gone too.

But one positive side to all this is that I can now tell the future where I
live. You can visit me at Morrison Street Apartments, Room #315.

12/8/99

Now I remember what I was going to write about yesterday, before I spilled my guts out on the page. The turn of the millennium has been on my mind lately with all of the biblical predictions and mystery surrounding it, as well as the computer worries. And if I don't forget about it, I'll try to make an entry on New Year's Day as close to the hour as possible.

So far my key word and symbol haven't appeared anywhere. I still believe that if I do meet someone from the future that I'll never know about it. They will just say "hi" as they pass me on the street.

You know what I just thought about? Since I've already said that contacting me might hinder the finishing of the book, I might have prevented any contact, just because of that statement alone. I may have set myself up for failure.

12/10/99

For some reason it slipped my mind to mention that I'm going to Austin, Texas to spend Christmas with my family. Earlier I called Calvin, my old college roommate who lives in Dallas, and he asked me if I could come visit him while I'm in Texas. I told him I could, but it would have to be a quick stop. Since I was thinking about it, I also asked him if he would edit a book I'm working on once I'm finished (without telling him what it was). He seemed very excited about it.

After talking to him, I made reservations with the airline. My flight leaves for Dallas on the 23rd and returns the 28th of this month. I'll have to drive down to Austin from DFW airport, but it's worth it. I like hanging out with his family.

12/12/99

What am I expecting from these time travelers anyway: money, guidance, fame, discovery, good fortune, insight, or maybe knowledge? A few weeks ago, I actually had the idea to make one of my journal entries with my pick of the lottery numbers for that weekend hoping that the future might be able to fix the outcome for me. My hope was that they wanted me to have money in order to publish this book, or some excuse like that.

My feelings toward this experiment have changed somewhat. Originally I was excited about the possibilities. It was something new and adventurous. But it's different now. I feel like there's a deep need inside of me for it to work. That if it turned out to be right then it would somehow validate my life.

12/15/99 11:43 PM

Yesterday I was watching a movie around 7:00 PM when there was a knock at my apartment door, almost like the light tapping of a key. Looking out my scratched and beat up peephole, I could see what looked like two guys, one in a white shirt and tie and the other, I believe, was dressed the same, except the second one had a sports jacket or cardigan over top. I knew immediately I wasn't expecting anyone dressed like that. So I sat back down and continued watching my movie. I was pretty sure these guys had noticed the light disappear behind the peephole, but I didn't care. They didn't knock again. Then the thought hit me, what if they were Mormons going door to door? I've seen a couple of them in the neighborhood on bicycles lately. But they shouldn't have been able to get in the building because of the gated door to the complex.

Make fun of them if you want, but the Mormons are very ingenious and organized.

In Salt Lake City, they have acquired some of the best genealogical records in the world. When a person needs to trace their ancestry, they usually contact the Mormons in Utah at some point. They probably know more about my family tree than I do.

Now here's the next thing to consider. I have sent off twice for the "free" Book of Mormon that they advertise over TV, because knowing about different religions is one of my pastimes. I ordered twice because my college roommate took my first copy for himself. It's a great system they have with the free books. When you call them, you obviously have to give them your name and address so they can send you your free copy. This benefits them in two ways. First, they have your address and can send you mail, or they can have a couple of people visit your door and talk to you.

Second, they can put your name and location in their enormous library, so now you're on file with them.

Do they keep these records in Utah just because they're bored? No, the Mormons believe that if you are not a part of their church that you can still be baptized into their church, even if you're not present. Don't quote me on this, but here's what I've heard: If you have a relative, distant or not, who belongs to the Mormon Church, then that relative can stand in for you and baptize you by proxy into their church. So you could be baptized in the Mormon Church whether you know it or not, and whether you like it or not.

But that leads up to what hit me shortly after the two guys left. With all the records of people, relatives, and addresses that are stored up in Utah, wouldn't they be the best source for tracking a person down? Maybe in the future they are the travel agency for time travelers, giving names, dates, and locations of anyone you need before you depart. And just maybe, when the Mormon's arrive at your door visiting, they're actually checking up on you for the future. Next time, I might just answer the door.

12/20/99

Going to Texas for Christmas will be a nice escape. And it will give me a chance to try another state for communication, just in case there is something wrong with California (no pun intended). Also the plane will be an interesting place for a log entry, as long as I can avoid anyone reading what I'm writing. I can just see the person next to me reading while I write something really strange like: "I'm here on the plane now, and I hope someone from the future comes up to me and announces himself or herself. Maybe the flight attendant could invite me to the bathroom for a mile high experience as a signal, or the plane could tip its wings one way and then the other as a signal from the pilot."

Yeah, I'll be careful when I write. I wouldn't want the plane grounded at the nearest airport and me questioned about my intentions. Not to mention having me locked away in a straight jacket and the book confiscated.

12/24/99

Because of the confines of the airplane, I was unable to make an entry while flying here. Today is Christmas Eve, and I am in Texas until the 28th of December. I arrived 12/23/99 noon at Dallas Fort Worth Airport. No matter what the circumstances are on the flight back, I will make some sort of entry, even if I have to go to the bathroom to make it happen.

I spent the night in Dallas with my old college roommate, Calvin. We went out and drank a lot and talked a lot, too. We started talking about language, and I happened to mention that the phrase "everything happens for a reason" is very popular in L.A. right now. But I told him that everyone who uses it seems to be pretty well off. None of them are missing limbs or short on cash. He thought that was interesting. Then we talked about predestination and a whole lot of other things. He's one of the only people that I can sit and really talk philosophy with. We got along great at the University. I miss the school days.

Presently I am in Austin, at my aunt's house, having Christmas. Most of my family is here, but my dad didn't make it. He left a key for me to the house but apparently he had to be out of town today on business.

Before I leave for California, I want to locate a couple of sturdy landmarks and write down an entry while inside. There may be a better chance of contact in Texas for one reason or another.

Only seven days left until the New Year. I'm reluctant to say new millennium because technically it isn't until 2001. There are now threats of terrorism, violence, riots, as well as the fear of Y2K making computers fail. It will be interesting to see if anything really happens.

12/25/99

I've been talking to a couple of my cousins, catching up on some things. I spent the night here at my aunt's instead of my dad's place. Everyone wants to come visit me in Los Angeles. People have this idea that it's amazing out there. I tell them that it's just like everywhere else except more exaggerated. If things are going good then it's really good, and if they're going bad then it's really, really bad.

I was talking to my Aunt Fran yesterday and the conversation turned to my dad. Without me saying anything, she began talking about how she wished he would treat me better. I was shocked. After a couple of glasses of wine, she got pretty talkative. Apparently my dad never wanted children, and it was a constant argument between my mom and him. They never talked about it before marriage (they married within eight months of meeting) and my mom just assumed he wanted kids. My mom was probably a little naïve, and she was definitely in love, so you can't completely judge her. Obviously, my aunt said, an accident happened and they had me. Fran said she talked to my mom about it and that it wasn't a trick my mom had pulled, it was really an accident. All the same my mom was happy about it, but my dad wasn't.

This morning my Aunt felt bad about telling me all of that. She said not to repeat it and made me promise that I wouldn't say anything under any circumstances. I have no reason to. But knowing does help me feel a little better. And I still want to talk to him about other things. Anyway, a bunch of us are going out later to 6th Street and visit some of the bars and hangouts here in town. I know it's not the best way to spend Christmas, but then again maybe it is. I'll go to my dad's place later for Christmas dinner.

12/26/99

I'm still awake and it's 2:00 AM at my dad's house. My dad came home earlier and we had dinner. He asked me how things were going in California, and I lied and told him it was pretty good. He wanted to know if I regretted studying Film instead of Physics, and I lied and said no. After dinner, he went to bed.

The house is nice and quiet right now, a definite change from the noisy streets of Los Angeles. With everything so peaceful, I've just been sitting and thinking. Earlier I saw a television program about time capsules for the next millennium. It got me thinking, this journal is a time capsule of sorts. I'm capturing places in time on a page, documenting my experiments and sealing them up in a book so future readers can trace them back and find me.

I took a few moments after writing that last sentence and sat here in the silence of the living room, just thinking and daydreaming. An old pendulum clock that stands in the corner ticked loudly and interrupted my thoughts. Almost mad at the noise, I stopped and looked at the clock. The sound overwhelmed me as the seconds ticked by, adding up into minutes, which create hours, then days.

12/26/99

I had to get out and away from everyone for a while, so I might as well go to a few places and do some experiments. The time is somewhere between 7:53 PM and 7:57 PM because the car clock reads four minutes faster than my watch. Here goes.

One of the best picks for landmarks is St. Mary's Cathedral. I'm just outside the one here in Austin. The weather is very cold, and I'm doing most of the writing from the car.

Here I am at 203 East 10th Street, where an old Catholic church stands. This is another sturdy structure with lasting significance in time. Blah, Blah, Blah, sometimes I get bored with my own writing.

Anyway, I'm sitting outside and it's 8:05 PM now. You'd think churches would be open today, especially since it's Sunday. I just thought I might have a chance at this one, but all the lights are off. Besides, it's the day after Christmas, so what am I thinking? This place won't be open the day after Christ's birthday. I'll try the door anyway just to satisfy my curiosity. Be right back.

Ok, I tried the door just now and I was right, it was locked. Maybe I'll try again tomorrow during the day.

12/27/99

Well, I spent the entire day today hanging out with family at my dad's, so I didn't get to try the church again. I probably shouldn't have, but I took some time out today and called Surrey to wish her a Merry Christmas. She's up in Wyoming for Christmas, where her parents live.

I was trying not to think about her too much, but my Aunt Fran kept asking me about her, and then everyone wanted to know why we'd broken up. I didn't know how to tell them that my best friend and my girlfriend were sleeping together behind my back, so I avoided answering any deep questions. But that got me thinking about her and I couldn't stop. So after several minutes of dialing half the number and hanging up, I called her. Her mom answered and asked how I was doing. I suspect Surrey hadn't told her how we'd broken up. Then she called for Surrey and gave her the phone. When Surrey found out it was me on the phone she got angry, then she asked what I'd said to her mother. I told her I didn't say anything, but I don't think Surrey believed me. When I told her I called to wish her Merry Christmas, she told me not to call there again, and then she hung up.

I should have never called her.

After that, I sat around in the living room feeling frustrated. Family kept coming in and going out, but pretty soon everyone was gone except my dad. Finally, after mustering the courage, I mentioned that I wanted to talk about some things. He said he didn't have time and then he left as well. So I decided to go out drinking by myself for a couple of hours, and now I feel much better.

12/28/99
My plane leaves later today and I still have to drive up to Dallas. I'm already packed and I told all the family goodbye. My dad was gone this morning when I got up, so I just left him a note. So, feeling bad about my lackluster performance with the journal while being here, I've decided to try the church again. Presently the time is 12:18 PM and I am outside the church. I'll try the door.

Three minutes later now and I'm inside. I don't think it's open to the public because no one is here and I entered through a side door. The front was locked.

It is beautiful in here. They've decorated the place for Christmas and the millennium with banners, Christmas trees, and a manger scene. The stained glass windows are wonderful.

According to the historical marker outside, this present structure was completed in 1874. It would be nice to be contacted by the right person here, but I'd better get out before the wrong person finds me and kicks me out. I probably shouldn't be in here.

12/28/99 12:32 PM
I've just driven a couple of miles away to finish the entry. That was the most excitement I've had making an entry. The structure was old and beautiful, and the chance of it lasting was fair, unless anarchy takes over, and then the idea I have about government and church buildings is shot down. It was also exciting because it felt like a good place for a contact. That, combined with the feeling of being caught in there and asked about my intentions, was exhilarating.

Not to be negative but what if the building burns down in a few years? They can't all burn down, can they? My guess is that the more churches and other lasting structures I visit the greater my chances become. The idea of anarchy or mass destruction has to be weighed in as well. Maybe for that scenario visiting a National Park would be a good variable in my experiment. If you go to the wilderness then it can't really change much, can it? Especially if it's protected at the present time. Even if it's built up with construction and then destroyed, it still remains a wilderness.

12/28/99
The time is 10:07 PM Texas time, on American Airlines flight 1121 from Dallas/Fort Worth to Long Beach airport.

12/28/99
It's now 10:30 PM California time, and I've landed. Just jotting down these notes before driving away from the airport. I was in seat 17D for half of the flight. With this entry coming after I've landed that pretty much rules out a contact. I let the stupid guy across the aisle exchange seats with me because he wouldn't stop talking across me to the girl on my right. So I wasn't in that seat very long. Sorry, it was a bad entry for a contact. But oddly enough it feels good to be back.

12/30/99

It's late Wednesday night or early Thursday morning, depending on how you look at it, but the time is 1:15 AM Thursday the 30th, and the date 01/01/00 is getting closer. I've been up late reading the last Time Magazine issue for this century. It's the December 31, 1999 Person of the Century issue, and Albert Einstein received the title. When I have more time, I want to read the issue in depth. It mentions "String Theory" and "M Theory" in a way that's easy to understand.

12/30/99

4:40 PM and, believe it or not, I'm on Orange Dr. and 2nd street again. I don't have my notebook with me, but I'm writing in a small pad I keep with me for ideas. Later, when I get home, I'll transfer them into my notebook. I'm writing because I just finished eating a burger and happened to see something interesting.

I was sitting in my car and, to my left across the street, a GQ looking guy was standing on the grass looking at me. I changed the radio station on my dash and pretended to ignore him. He proceeded to stand there just beyond my peripheral view for a few minutes then he walked to a tree, within my view, but still on the other side of the street. He faced the tree and leaned both his palms against it. He didn't stretch or look around, he just faced the tree propping himself up with both hands.

My creative imagination kicked in, and I thought about a group of people in the future who lack knowledge of the past, but still have the time travel capabilities. Their only link to the fashion of this time period is a 1996 fall issue of J. Crew magazine that has survived. So they dress their best man for the job in an outfit to match the time period and send him back to Orange Dr. in 1999.

Lost and confused by the trauma of time travel, he stands on the street corner, not remembering what he was sent here for. In order to get his bearings, he gravitates to the only familiar object in sight, a tree, which he remembers seeing in a museum once in his childhood. He goes over and leans on the tree to collect his thoughts, and focuses for just a moment. Before he can remember that his purpose for coming here was to contact me, I get out of my Jeep and go back to work.

12/31/99

Time left in the Millennium is slowly being snuffed out. At 8:45 PM, I am at home in my apartment about to leave for Allen's house in order to count out the last seconds of the year with two or three other people. I will try to make an entry as soon as possible after the New Year rolls in.

01/01/00
The time is 2:02 AM. The first day of the new millennium, and I'm at my place all alone. I just left Allen's place and came back to make an entry. Nothing has changed I suppose, just the date on the calendar.

All the same, this is a wonderful moment to be able to log a journal entry at the dawn of a new millennium. Maybe tomorrow, when my wits are together and sobriety has set in, I can make another entry with greater insight and depth.

01/01/00 11:32 AM
Well, I believe my insight was better this morning at 2:02 AM than now. There's no reason for this entry really, except I enjoy writing down the new date, it looks very nice.

01/01/00
It's about 3:00 in the afternoon. I know it's my third entry today, but I can't stop thinking about people seeing into the past and watching me. But assuming the capability does become available and they can watch us, me in particular, then that means they can see everything I do all hours of the day. In a way it's a scary idea, all-seeing all-knowing and maybe keeping records or videotaping it. For the sake of posterity, I hope they're keeping it all to themselves and not putting it on some futuristic talk show.

01/01/00
The last time ever (I think) I will make an entry with those wonderful digits 01/01/00. Right now it is 11:10 PM and closing on midnight, ending the first full day of the new millennium. Today has been very philosophical for me concerning time, probably because the year 2000 seems to embody the idea of time and change.

A blurb on the news a couple of days ago told about the oldest woman in the world, 119 years old, and all she wanted was to see the new millennium. She died two days before it arrived. Nothing is guaranteed.

It makes you stop and consider how long each of us will live. What will our children become? Will we die tomorrow? Then there are all the personal questions, like, do I have a purpose here? Am I doing everything I can to fulfill my goals, or am I trying too hard and not enjoying life? We respect time and we fear it, too. It seems to have a hold on everything that we hold dear.

Charles Kingsley has a poem that I read earlier today. Somehow it takes all these ideas and, for a moment, helps me understand them.

YOUNG AND OLD

When all the world is young, lad,
And all the trees are green;
And every goose a swan, lad,
And every lass a queen,
Then hay for boot and horse, lad,
And round the world away;
Young blood must have it's course, lad,
And every dog his day.

When all the world is old, lad,
And all the trees are brown;
And all the sport is stale, lad,
And all the wheels run down;
Creep home, and take your place there,
The spent and maimed among:
God grant you find one face there,
You loved when all was young.

01/06/00

Today I asked Allen a question at work. Upon hearing me, he said he experienced a déjà vu. This, of course, is the phenomenon where you feel as if you are experiencing something for a second time, or feeling like you have been there before. The dictionary defines it as "the illusion of having previously experienced something actually being encountered for the first time."

Scientists have some tenuous ideas of what could cause the anomaly (such as slow impulses to the brain) but my opinion is more interesting. I think we have been given a second chance at something in life. Maybe someone in the future, or providence, has done a "restart" for us and put us in a position to change something. The "restart" causes the déjà vu, and for a second we remember something familiar.

Maybe it's silly. But it's more romantic than the scientific version.

01/08/00

My boss cut back my hours today and told me I wasn't selling enough.
Several customers had complained to him that I seemed uninterested in
what I was doing. Of course, doing the same thing every day is going
to get old. And how enthusiastic do you need to be to sell cameras?

My job is to know the equipment and inform the customers on the best
choice for their needs. Why do I need to be extremely happy about
that? You just do it. Anyway, I'm on a type of probation to see if my
attitude improves, and, if so, then I can get all my hours back.

01/30/00

Just past midnight, so that actually makes it Sunday morning the 30th. Unfortunately, I've been so busy at work that I haven't made an entry in a while. I've probably been a little depressed, too, but the book is always on my mind.

I need to find out what to do next. What level can I take it to that I haven't already? Should I try doing the same things I've been doing, except more often and in different places? There has to be something I'm not thinking of that could end this and give me either a positive or negative confirmation. What do I need? If I could foretell the future, or just know what happens with time travel, that would help. Where does it begin? What country or state tests it first? How far back will they go in time? What are they looking for in a contact?

Someone has to be in control of the time machine or lab. Maybe it's just one individual, a private inventor. How could I tempt the man who controls the button to the time machine? Could I get him pissed off, or maybe encourage him? Dare him, maybe, to test me? Insult him or his mother, if that would help? What is his name? If I'm writing this sentence right now, and he's in the future reading it right now, then maybe he could just mouth his name. Whisper it under his breath as he reads this, and then, maybe, if I sit still long enough, I can hear him.

02/05/00

Well, I no longer take my lunch breaks on the corner of Orange Dr. and 2nd street anymore. My job moved to a different location, so those other streets are a thing of the past. Isn't it strange how quickly things become a part of the past? One day I'm sitting eating lunch in my Jeep and decide to write an entry in my book, shortly thereafter it becomes history.

With this change in location, I've been thinking about cause and effect again, and have more questions. Does every little thing we do today change tomorrow's outcome like a domino effect? Do our actions today, even the smallest ones, determine the outcome of the rest of our lives? Or is it more like predestination?

My friend in Dallas is named John Calvin, after the leader of the Protestant Reformation. John Calvin (the reformer) started what is known as Calvinism, the main belief of which is predestination. While I was home, I talked to him about time theories (I didn't tell him about the book), and he brought up predestination. Predestination says that God has already planned out everything that will happen to mankind. True Calvinists believe that God planned out everything before he even created the universe, even who's going to heaven and who's not. Aside from the heaven and hell thing, this philosophy resembles my theory of everything in time being unchangeable. "Set in stone," is the phrase I used.

The opposite of predestination would probably be the idea of a domino effect, better known as Chaos theory in scientific circles. Chaos theory says that small occurrences can lead to very large changes over a period of time. Popularly known as "the butterfly effect," it says that a butterfly flapping it's wings in one country, causes a chain of events that ultimately makes it rain in another country.

Is this an irrational theory, though? Would you want to believe in a theory that says that shaving tomorrow instead of tonight before bed, will change your entire life?

Say that one day you shave in the morning, instead of the night before, and you're so tired that you cut yourself with the razor. You shave slower now, and this makes you two minutes behind where you would have been, had you done it the night before. Now when you head out for work the guy that would have been behind you in traffic is in front of you and going very slow, so you swerve to go around him and subsequently side swipe a car. Now you have interfered with the lives of all the people behind you that are caught in your traffic jam, all because you didn't shave the night before.

It's difficult to tell what could happen. We can't conduct this experiment exactly the same way twice without shaving at one point in time and following the person through life, then winding the clock back and shaving at another time to see if one variable makes a difference.

Who knows? Maybe we are better off, or even alive today, because of that one mistake.

02/06/00
Today I have been reading through some of the past entries, and I came across the one made on 12/28/99 inside the church in Texas. For some reason I wondered what would happen if I was able to travel back in time and visit myself.

The idea is conceivable because the technology could be just a few years away. I mean I never thought I would live to see the day that cloning would be achieved. My grandmother occasionally tells about reading space travel comic books, and everyone thought it was ludicrous to go to the moon until a man actually went there. What if, within my lifetime, travel through time becomes possible, and I still have this notebook to refer back to? This would even eliminate the need for the book to reach the masses.

I had never considered that. Maybe I could even be the creator of the first machine. That would give me complete control.

Ok, going back to my original idea, what if I had the chance to travel back in time when I reached the age of sixty, because of advances in science? If I could do it, would I choose to go back to 12/28/99 and step up to my younger self and announce my arrival? Let's say I didn't even reveal who I was, but just walked in and sat down. Would I do that to myself? I think I'd be too afraid of jeopardizing my work.

But let's say that this book goes nowhere and by the age of sixty I know that it goes nowhere, then there would be no need to worry about the book's completion. Still, I don't believe I would do it, as tempting as it may be. The old Chaos theory comes into play here. How would it affect the rest of my life?

02/07/00

With the day off, I'm out trying more locations. This time I'm sitting at the Central Library in downtown Burbank at a small row of desks, just to the left, as you walk in the left doors. I hate being this specific when I write but it's the only way to do it. The clock on the wall says 1:30 PM. I'm wearing a gray T-shirt with a blue-checkered long-sleeve shirt over it, sleeves rolled up.

Just to add a variable in this experiment I would like to see a woman with a hat drop a couple of books as she walks near my desk, but only if she's a contact.

That sounds horribly boring. You know what? Let's change it up a little here. If I'm going to make a request it might as well be a good one. I'm tired of all these pseudo coincidences. This time I'm going to make a grand request where there can be no mistaking the connection. Here's what I want to see, a cat running through the doors of the library and the owner chasing the cat. No! I've got something better. A monkey. A monkey with a green sweater running in the door of the library being chased by a fat man with only swim shorts on. Hell, I don't care if he's wearing nothing at all, just give me the fat man and the monkey.

Now there's an entry for you. If the future can supply that as a sign then we're in business and I can just stop writing this book now. I swear, I wouldn't need any further confirmation than that. I might need a psychiatrist, but not further confirmation.

The cross streets here are Glen Oaks and Orange Grove. I don't know why streets with the name Orange keep coming up but, be assured, I'm not intentionally doing this.

Last night I saw the movie "The Matrix" again. The story is amazing, as well as the effects, editing, etc. The ideas in the film aren't new, much of it can be found in Plato's writings and other literary works. The depth of the film, though, and its seemingly flawless detail of the story's philosophy are lingering in my mind today.

The time is nearly 1:45 PM, and I'm still waiting for my fat man and monkey to show up. You may think I'm joking about this entry, but I'm not. I said I needed to try something different, and this is about as different as it can get. Actually, I don't care if a fat man or a fat woman chases the monkey at this point. They wouldn't even have to be naked. As a matter of fact, I don't care if someone comes over to me, taps me on the shoulder and says, "Hey, I'm from the future, I bet your name is Jason!"

The time is 1:52 PM right now, and I'm still waiting.

Ok, that's it. I'm out of here. The clock on the wall now says 2:00 PM, and no one has tapped me on the shoulder and no monkeys have come through the door. Even though there was a fat guy that walked in with an ugly pair of shorts and a T-shirt.

Anyway, I'm leaving.

02/10/00

My dad called me today. I got off the phone with him just a little while
ago. It kind of surprised me. He actually asked me how I was doing.
We talked a little, and I asked him if he enjoyed Christmas, being busy
with work and all. He said that he had a good time.

But what he really called to tell me was that he is moving to Chicago.
Not on a business venture, or on a whim, but because he's going to
marry a lady up there. This was the first I'd heard of it. He has been
dating her for quite a while apparently. Actually, I'm just assuming
they've been dating a while, he didn't say how long. But she was in
town over Christmas, from what he said, and he didn't even tell me
about her or introduce me.

I know his life is his own, and I have nothing to do with it, but I had
assumed that if he had found someone, especially with mom passing
away and all, that he would tell me or at least ask my opinion of her. I
suppose I'm being selfish. But I don't know.

And maybe I've read Hamlet too many times, but shouldn't he have
given it more time? How soon should you remarry after losing a
spouse? I'm not saying that he didn't really love Mom, but, I don't
know.

Anyway, after telling me about his new fiancé, I realized that all the
pleasantries of the phone conversation were just sugar coating to
prepare me for the news. He told me he already had a buyer for the
house and that he would be moving within the week. That house is the
house I grew up in. Then he acted like he had to be somewhere and cut
the conversation short.

Part of me had always hoped things between my dad and me would
change and that I might find a little place of my own in Austin to be
near him. But that's all changed now. My Aunt Fran would be happy
to see me move back, but that's not quite the same.

02/11/00

If I'm wrong and time travel is truly impossible to accomplish, then all of this work I'm doing is in vain. Not only that, but it also means that time only passes us once. Each moment in our life, each event, first impressions, this very moment, all of it happens only once and then it's gone. What do we do with it?

02/12/00 7:00PM
What the hell, I did it. I went out and bought three lottery tickets tonight. The numbers for the first ticket are:

11 * 22 * 23 * 30 * 44 * 49

And yes, I am double-checking the numbers. The second set is:

11 * 16 * 18 * 21 * 31 * 50

The third and final set of lottery numbers is:

10 * 15 * 32 * 42 * 44 * 51

If I'm not mistaken, the drawing will be tonight sometime after 10:00 PM. This is for the California drawing, just so no one is confused. The reason I bought three tickets? Variables of course, just in case one set works better for some reason.

As I was leaving work today, I had planned on stopping by the farmer's market and buying a ticket, but when I arrived they were closed. Next, I went to Sav-On's grocery store. Needing some gum anyway, I bought a pack and asked the clerk if they sold lottery tickets. He told me they didn't, but he said there was a 7-11 up the street that did. He handed me my change and said to me, "You must have had a dream." I laughed and, being agreeable, replied, "Yeah." Then suddenly I remembered back to the dream I had last night. I turned to the clerk again and said, "Actually I did."

Last night I had a dream that I won a large sum of money, I believe it was $100,000. I had completely forgotten about it because the events of the day had pushed it to the back of my mind.

02/13/00 1:13 PM
Well I finally found the lottery numbers hidden away in the Sunday paper. Even though it would have been nice to win, I didn't. And truthfully, I wasn't expecting to win. That's why I was in no real hurry to find the numbers. All the same, it's another experiment achieved.

On my desk there's that copy of Time Magazine with Albert Einstein just staring at me from the cover. After seeing the lottery numbers, I found myself talking out loud to his picture. Mr. Einstein basically sat and stared at me and didn't say anything, but I could feel him thinking about my questions. He probably knows the answers, but he's not telling.

02/29/00

It is leap year 2000. The time is 7:35 PM, and (no surprise) I've been wondering again about people in the future. I walked through a brand-new grocery store today near my apartment, and I wondered what the same area of land looked like 500 years ago. Then I considered what it would look like 500 years from today. This made me wonder about the people 500 years from today, or even farther than that, 2000 years, 3000 years, from today. What if someone from that far away really contacts me? What will the people from that time period be like? Will they have amazing technology or be physically different? Considering how language has evolved since Shakespeare, or even further back, would they even be able to speak to me?

Let's shock ourselves and imagine the human race, if they're still called that, one million years in the future. Now, what if it takes that long to create time travel?

Imagine that someone digs up the back yard where you buried this book one million years earlier, and translates it to discover that it's a book written to the future and to time travelers in particular. They take the book to the correct people, and in turn, decide to contact me. Now, what would happen if two species, separated by a gap of one million years, come together? Of course, this is all playing games, but imagine, if there is even the slightest chance of it happening, what would be the result?

03/01/00

It is ten minutes past midnight and I have been sitting up for the last hour looking at old photos of my family and thinking back on my youth. There's this one photo in particular of my granddad, an old black and white that I can't stop staring at. The funny thing is, being a photographer, I wonder who took this picture. It's a professional photo, so I know it wasn't family. But if that unknown person hadn't taken the picture, I might not have it in my hands.

I've thought about quitting work and starting my own photography business. My sole marketing idea would focus on creating "time capsules" for families. The capsule would come with photos, a disc of the scanned negatives, and some type of protective container to put it all in. Then, years later someone could pull that can out of the closet, or wherever it's been stored, and cherish it. The photographs will have traveled through time, just like this picture of my grandfather has.

You could say, just for the heck of it, that we all travel forward in time at a rate of one second per second. But it's not such a silly idea, because this photo of my grandfather has slowly traveled through time and has arrived here with me.

05/04/00 3:20 PM

I'm sitting in my Jeep on Colgate in Hollywood between Fairfax and Edinburgh. I haven't written in a while because I've been kind of down. The days I have off I can't seem to get out of bed and end up sleeping most of the day. Today my boss talked about laying me off. Days like today make me so exhausted with my mundane life that every genetic strand of my body cries out for this experiment to work.

05/05/00

I have made a decision that could be my last attempt at bringing this book to a close. My work with this journal is approaching ten months now with no perceivable results. Exaggerated efforts at this point, I believe, are better than no efforts at all. That is why I have asked work to give me a week off at the end of May, from 05/21/00 to 05/28/00. I have decided to go north to Yosemite National Park. The Yosemite calendar on my wall has been tempting me with pictures of the Park's beautiful surroundings. And I think a little escape would be good for me right now. Of course, there is a plan behind this trip to Yosemite, besides getting away from the hustle of L.A. life.

Looking over my past journal logs the other day, I found something interesting that helped initiate this vacation. On 8/11/99, I made a journal entry while listening to the radio. The musical piece that was played was by Bedrich Smetana, and it was called The Moldau. The dictionary says Moldau is "a river in Czechoslovakia flowing north through the Bohemian Forest to the Elbe, 270 miles long." What's different about this? Well, a lot of rivers in the world flow from north to south, with the exception of some that flow north. Strange as it may seem, I found myself connecting this with my feelings about doing an experiment in the wilderness, and that's how I arrived at the idea. Yosemite is a wilderness, and it's north of here, and that's how I made the fragile connection. Sure, it's not much, but I thought with nowhere else to go I might as well try. Anyway, if I'm wrong, the only downfall is a week's vacation in Yosemite.

We can idly sit by and watch things happen or jump in and cause them to happen. A few years back, I came up with a great maxim for life that goes like this: We only regret two things in life, the things we do and the things we don't do. I would rather regret having done a few things in life than regret never having attempted them at all.

05/06/00

Well, the second half of today was spent looking through the bookstore, finding everything possible on Yosemite National Park. It should be noted that there are hundreds of books about parks, and the ones on Yosemite are full of pictures.

I walked away with a modest number of books, four to be exact, that contain maps, places to take pictures from, average temperatures during each month of the year, wildlife, you name it. This one book that I'm looking at says temperatures for Yosemite, during the time I'll be there, will range from lows of 42 degrees Fahrenheit up to a high of around 73. The rain outlook is a 20% possibility of wet weather with a 70% chance of a sunny day. Don't ask me what they did with the other 10%, I'm just reading the book.

Sounds like nice weather if you ask me. "Jacket wearing weather," makes me feel good, especially when I'm outside enjoying nature. When I was a kid, the only weather I would willingly go camping in was mildly cold. Cold offers fewer bugs, fewer snakes, the need to build a fire, and a feeling of ruggedness that seems necessary when camping.

One of the books has a phone number for the hotel that sits in the Yosemite Valley. It's called the Ahwahnee Hotel. I'll call them later and set aside a room for that week. If my computer was up and running, I could get on the Internet and find out a lot more information. Oddly enough, I'm completely happy not having my computer, and most of the time, I don't even watch television. Writing on paper has become an addiction for me these past few months. I don't know if I'll ever switch back.

05/06/00

After that last entry, I called the reservation number and asked about prices and locations in the Yosemite Valley. The Ahwahnee appears to be the most lavish and accommodating hotel in the park. It's pricey, but I thought I would stay there the first night or two and then move over to the more reasonable Yosemite Lodge for the rest of my stay. I've got a little room on a couple of credit cards, so I might as well use them on this trip. The Ahwahnee sounds very interesting because it's been there since 1927.

There was also a place called Curry Village that housed it's guests in a "canvas walled cabin," which sounds like a glorified name for a tent. They have plenty of vacancies at all the locations. The lady on the phone said I could switch my accommodations later if needed. So the reservations are made, first at the Ahwahnee, and then later I'll switch to Yosemite Lodge.

05/07/00

Today I went to the music store in search of The Moldau on CD. I thought that buying it would give me some inspiration. I wanted some new music anyway.

So, with the help of some very astute guys in the classical section, I found the seemingly elusive recording. These guys also gave me more information about the music, specifically that The Moldau is only a small part of a larger work that the composer, Bedrich Smetana, called Ma Vlast (or My Fatherland). Ma Vlast consists of symphonic poems that symbolize Smetana's homeland of Czechoslovakia (That's what the CD sleeve says).

I've listened to the piece twice, since I got home, and I love it. It has a very pastoral and natural sound to it. Almost like swirling waters flowing down a river, which I'm sure is no coincidence.

When I get to Yosemite, I'll have to find a quiet river and write one of my entries while listening to the babbling waters flow by. This is going to be very nice.

05/20/00

Tomorrow's the big day for me, and I'm very excited about it. Since they're giving me next week off, I had to work today, even though it's Saturday. Otherwise, I could have been on the road already. That's ok, though, I probably won't leave until Sunday night so that traffic can calm down from the weekend.

This town is very odd to me. People in Los Angeles all leave the city on Saturday morning in order to hide out for a single day, and then return Sunday night. For the life of me, I don't see how any of them enjoy it. Such a short vacation, and most of their time is spent in traffic. A lot of them end up in a popular spot with the same crowd of people they were trying to escape from.

05/21/00
Today I am very happy. The time is 2:00 PM, and I'm close to leaving.
All of my stuff is scattered on my bed in no particular order and ready
to go into suitcases. My packing skills have been honed to perfection
from all of the traveling back and forth to Texas.

I love road trips so much that I can't explain it in words. This is going
to be a little strange, though, because I'm going by myself.

I might stay at a motel in Fresno tonight. I may not want to drive the
entire way non-stop. It's about 6 hours to Fresno and then 2 more
hours into the heart of the Park. To be honest I'm a little apprehensive
about going on a long trip by myself, it's a little unnerving when you
think about it. If anything happens to the car, or if I lose my wallet,
then what will I do? I'm sure I can handle myself, but there won't be
the security of having another head to help think through situations.
And then there's the silence. Not talking to anyone for the six to eight
hour drive could get the best of me. I bought some books on tape at the
book store the other day, so maybe that will give me some relief.

Looking over my supplies earlier, I realized I could run out of paper, so
I went out and bought some filler paper to thicken up my notebook. I
also purchased three fresh pens, in case of an emergency, and some
film for taking pictures of those beautiful waterfalls. And, just for the
fun of it, my harmonica is packed up and ready to go with me.
I should be out of here within the hour so that I'm not driving too
much at night.

05/21/00
Well, that took a little longer than I expected because the time is now
5:15 PM. Finally, I have my Jeep packed and I'm sitting in the driver's
seat ready to leave. I spent the last couple of hours running around
town getting things together. I bought a sleeping bag at a camping
store in case I camp out, bought some snacks for the long drive, then I
went and bought what they call a "phone in a box" at 7-11. It's a neat
little idea because I needed a phone for security on the trip, and they
sell them ready to go across the counter.

Now, one last look at the map to make sure my route is good before heading out. The best way to Fresno should be getting on the 170 freeway, right next to my apartment, and taking it a few miles up to Interstate 5. The 5 will take me all the way into Bakersfield, and then, after Bakersfield, I can get on the 99 and go all the way to Fresno. Tomorrow, after I get up and have breakfast, my favorite meal of the day, I'll probably take the 41 into Yosemite Park.

Getting to Fresno shouldn't take six hours, but if by chance it does then it will be close to midnight before I arrive, and I don't have a room yet. Motel 6 or La Quinta should do the trick for a savvy traveler like myself.

I listened to The Moldau once more before leaving, and I'm inspired. Already I feel better, in anticipation of whatever may lie up in Yosemite or anywhere in between. Wish me good luck.

05/21/00

The time is 7:02 PM. I've stopped to fill up with gas, something not planned ahead of time, obviously. I'm not sure what small town I'm in, or if you would even call this a town, but I'm estimating it will only be another 20 or 30 minutes to get to Bakersfield. I got myself a cup of coffee and a cinnamon roll from inside the filling station. There's something about the road and driving that makes me crave coffee. Maybe I should have become a truck driver to make a living, or maybe I was one in a former life, if you believe that kind of thing. Still, there's something about driving that frees up the soul and makes you feel good, especially driving at night. California has perfect night weather.

Here's something strange. Since leaving my apartment I've had two déjà vu's. Once, when I looked down and adjusted the radio, I had a flash of déjà vu and it lasted for a long time. Even when the disc jockey started talking, I could have sworn I had heard what he was saying before. The effect was so intense and real that as it faded away, it felt like I was re-entering my own body. I know it sounds strange, but I'm just trying to explain it as thoroughly as possible. I think it's the strongest one I've ever experienced.

The other one was weak. At one point I looked over and saw a barn with cattle standing around it and had a quick flash of having seen that setting before, kind of like a snapshot going off in my head. For all I know, they could have used that barn with cattle around it in a hundred western movies. But the radio thing is completely inexplicable.

Well, the coffee is almost gone, and my nerves are telling me I'd better stop writing and start driving, or else get out and run to Yosemite.

05/21/00 7:48 PM

Bakersfield, California: as big as life. It looks like a nice place to drive through, but I guess I'll have to stay the night. When I got into Bakersfield, I noticed my car pulling to the right and thought my wheels might be out of alignment, something I wouldn't notice until driving a long distance. So I pulled over on the north side of Bakersfield, just as I was exiting town, and examined my passenger side tire. It wasn't just low, it was looking close to flat. So I put some of that fix-your-tire-in-a-can-stuff in the tire and it aired the thing right up. But I wasn't going to drive down lonely highways at night on the hunch that some guy in a factory gave me the right proportions of air to goop in that can. A Motel 6 was at the next exit down, so I stopped for a room, and now I'm sitting in my car about to go in and check out the pad. I really don't know what I'll do since the coffee is still running through my system. Maybe they'll have a movie channel to watch.

05/22/00 9:30 AM

Finally, at about 1:00 this morning, the coffee died down enough for me to sleep. Before going to bed I asked for an 8:00 wake up call, which, in hindsight, was smart because otherwise I would have slept 'til noon.

After getting ready, I paid a visit to Milt's coffee shop across the street for breakfast and more coffee, and, on the way back to the motel, I checked the Jeep tire to see how it was holding up. Everything looked ok, so I'm guessing it should make the trip. The Jeep is loaded up, so all that's left to do is double check that my stuff is out of the room and to pay the bill. I swear I like this traveling and living in a motel thing too much. Maybe I should change careers and become a traveling salesman or something. As all things do, I'm sure it would get old, just like any other job, and soon I would hate the road and the smell of coffee.

05/22/00 11:33 AM

Tulare, what a strange name for a town. I wonder if it's pronounced (too lahr e) or maybe (to lar) or possibly (to Larry). Whichever it is, I dare not ask the locals or they may find that I'm an out-of-towner and ruin my car. That's right, my car is lined up to go into a garage. It seems as though that fix-a-stuff wore off after a few miles and my tire began leaking air. So now I'm taking a break in a restaurant just down the street and I can see out the window that my car hasn't moved from it's original spot yet. It's been close to an hour now, and there seems to be a lot of people with car trouble today.

Maybe this trip is jinxed, and I'm not supposed to be going to Yosemite. Or I could look at it from the standpoint of my childhood pastor who would say, "If the devil's beatin' you down son, you've gotta be doing something right." Of course, I don't want to provoke the devil here, but it does seem at times that I've fallen into an evil vortex.

I never completely understood that whole idea of the good people being beaten down by the devil. You would think that if the devil wants you on his side, then he would take great care in treating you nicely in order to entice you. If the devil's plan was to make me like him more by beating me, then it never worked, the supposed beatings only made me hate him more. Throw some money in my face or introduce me to a pretty, amiable, girl, and then you have my attention. But that's too obvious, what an intelligent being should do (assuming the devil is intelligent) is entice you with the thing you desire the most but suspect the least. To catch me personally, by my most vulnerable lust, he would probably give me super wisdom and intelligence, slowly, and in a subtle way, then have people compliment me on my wise decisions. Then he would twist my newly found pride in knowledge to his advantage. Before long he would have me believing I could do no wrcng while doing nothing but wrong. Just like the poison arsenic, which kills slowly and without detection, he would have me dead before I knew anything was wrong.

Anyway, how did I get on this subject? I can tell that getting out and doing something, even having a destination to drive to, has made me feel freer, and I'm writing a lot more. The scenery just outside of L.A. was beautiful with the rolling hills covered with prairie grass, but now it's become a repetition of small lonely towns obscured by trees planted along the highway. But being out of L.A., and the smog, changes the way I feel. And that has to account for half of my newly acquired sanity.

I'd better go check on my car.

05/22/00
I have to tell you about this. My car wasn't ready when I checked earlier, so I went back to the restaurant to get dessert and waited, since I had a perfect view of my car from there.

A little more than an hour ago, a man somewhere in his late 80s came up and asked if he could sit down beside me. I said, "yes," out of politeness. He started talking to me just as I finished eating. He didn't seem like a bum, and he didn't ask me for anything, but still he had the appearance of a transient. At first I shook my head "yes" to whatever he was saying just to be agreeable, like you do when you're pretending to listen to someone. But then he started making sense, and my attention peaked. He talked about when he was younger, and how things were different then than they are now: society, technology, attitudes, etc. His voice had a tone of kindness yet hinted of disparity, like he was hurting from the inescapable progression of time. I started asking questions at this point, and he began talking about a girl he used to be in love with.

His name was William, and he was ten years old when this girl moved into his hometown. He said that she was an only child and didn't know anyone. He mentioned that back in those days if you moved to a town that you weren't born in, you never really got accepted there. No matter how old you lived to be in that "new" town, everyone still referred to you as the newcomer. But he liked her, and they got to be good friends. They went to the same school and neither one of them made many friends with the other schoolmates. He was kind of quiet as a kid, and he got picked on by some of the other boys at school, but he didn't think much about it because that's how things went back then. He told me that this girl was shy herself but outgoing enough to make life interesting. So he and this girl, I think he said her name was Margaret, got to liking each other as time went on. Yes, her name was definitely Margaret, I remember now.

By the age of fifteen, their hormones were starting up and they started to see each other as more than just friends. They had made a decision to be boyfriend and girlfriend. They did everything together: play, school, homework; and people started saying that they would get married some day. They were both the same age, and at seventeen they decided they should get married, because after graduation they would have to go on to school or find work and they couldn't see not being together. So they made plans that in July, after graduation, they would get married.

As July approached, Margaret started getting weak and having fainting spells. Some people said it was the heat, others nerves, and then there were rumors that she was pregnant. William worried about her and thought something bad might be wrong. Some of the women told him he was over exaggerating and that she would be fine, but he didn't listen to them. After much arguing and discussion with her parents,

William took her to a doctor in a town about a hundred miles away to have her examined.

They arrived, and the doctor ran tests on her, which William admitted, were crude in comparison to today's tests. Thinking that something was wrong, but hoping for the best, William was ready for a bad diagnosis of some kind, but the doctors said that Margaret seemed fine. They told her to stay out of the sun and rest for a few days. They also told her she wasn't pregnant.

So the two arrived back in town the next day, and the parents wanted to know the results. When they told everyone she was fine, some people started to think the trip was all a ruse to get out of town for a night, and still others thought she had gotten an abortion. Margaret rested for a couple of days and then the two of them continued their plans for the wedding, with her parents now suspicious of William.

Two weeks before the wedding, Margaret hit her head after a fainting spell and had to go to the hospital. When she arrived, the doctor–on-call examined her. He looked at the bruise she sustained on her head from the fall. From there they started running exams on her and found that she had cancer of the brain. The doctor took the family into a room and told them that there was no way to stop the cancer because there was too much, and it was too far advanced. William wanted to be the one to tell Margaret about the situation, and he did.

The wedding continued as planned and the two got married, knowing that they wanted to spend every piece of time together that they could. William knew that one of Margaret's dreams was to go to Florida, so he took some of his savings and upgraded the honeymoon. They rode first class on a train there and back, and stayed for a week in a nice hotel. When they returned, William only took a part-time job so he could be with his wife. He used his savings to help out where the job money fell short.

It was only a few months later that the inevitable came, and Margaret fainted for the last time. William didn't tell me much detail about the end, and I didn't really want to know. He choked up and probably couldn't have explained much else anyway. He just kept talking about how wonderful she was and how he never found anyone else after that.

We shook hands as he was leaving, and foolishly I asked him if he needed any money for breakfast, still thinking he might be homeless, but he kindly refused. The man truly was still heartbroken after all these years. It must be both amazing and frightening to find someone you love so completely, someone who changes your life forever, and then to lose them. The chance of finding such a person is incalculable; the thought of losing them shortly thereafter would be unimaginable. How could you go on? Anyway, when he got up to leave, I almost asked him to stay longer, but I knew there was no reason. My car was sitting in a different parking place, so I assumed it was finished.

My car is driving fine now, and I've been sitting here in the parking lot of a hotel writing all this down before I forget any of it. It was truly a wonderful experience for me to have met him. My extended trip seems to have exhausted my funds, so I need to stop at an ATM machine to get cash, and then I'm out of here. I see a bank sign just up the street.

05/22/00
This is very weird, and I don't know exactly how to write about it, or even if I should. Suddenly I feel very ill. My head is a little swimmy, so I'm going to lean back in my car seat for a second and see if it dissipates.

Ok, I'm feeling a little better now, but still somewhat disturbed. As I was going up to the bank's ATM machine, I suddenly felt a strange sensation come over me, like I had walked into a wall of emotions. It was like a déjà vu of sorts, but it wasn't a normal déjà vu. The bank didn't look familiar and neither did the ATM. Explaining the experience might not be easy, but it seems that most of it was felt and not seen. Kind of like those distorted dreams where the feelings of the dream override the visual. Something like telling a friend you had a dream about being at the White House, but it didn't look like the White House, it looked more like your garage.

That's what happened to me just now. Feelings of sadness washed over me. As if I was watching someone I loved drown and was unable to save them. A knot swelled up in my throat and I almost started to cry. I couldn't make it stop. I leaned against the ATM and gasped until finally it went away. I know it all sounds strange, but that's the only way I can explain what happened. Maybe William's story hit me harder than I thought. Now I'm apprehensive about driving the rest of the way, and I don't feel well. I'll drive a little while and see if it changes.

05/22/00

It's been about thirty minutes now, and I've been driving around town not sure if I should leave or not. I started to just leave a few minutes ago, but now I'm at the edge of town pulled over on the side of the road. I absolutely don't want to spend the night here, but I don't feel good enough to drive on.

At the last exit, before pulling over, I saw a dry cleaner's sign with one of those strange sayings that read: "You are creating it all, nobody else is doing it to you." Very odd.

My conclusion is that it won't hurt me to spend the night. Besides, if I follow the advice of the dry cleaners sign, then I am creating it all, no one else is doing it to me.

05/23/00

The time is 8:00 AM, and I'm up and about to leave. Last night, I slept better than I have in a long time. I stayed the night at the Comfort Suites, but I don't want to stay another minute here. This morning my dizziness is gone, and I feel great. Last night, I called the Ahwahnee Hotel in Yosemite and told them I would need to change my reservation to today and they were very understanding. They had several rooms available, so they could afford to understand.

Just for the record, I have to tell you that I turned on the news early this morning and saw a report of a wreck that happened last night. Several cars were involved in the accident on the highway where I was when I turned around. I probably would have been stuck in a traffic jam last night anyway, so that makes me feel better about the overnight stay. Anyway, enough said. I'm out of here, and hopefully my next entry will be from Yosemite Park.

05/23/00

Yeah, I'm finally inside the park! The lady at the entrance said it's necessary to stop here, at Wawona, to get gas because there are no more gas stations in the park, so I'm filling up. Still, it's about 30 or 45 more minutes 'til I reach my destination. I didn't know that once you enter the park, it takes nearly an hour to get to the Yosemite Valley. The lady at the entrance said the entire park was about the size of Rhode Island.

In the past couple of hours, I've seen more dust devils and winding roads than ever before in my life. I stopped in Fresno for something to eat at McDonalds, and, shortly after that, the winding roads began.

I'm actually proud of myself for going this far on a vacation by myself. Until not long ago, I was afraid to do things on my own, especially taking long trips. Now that I'm here, though, all alone in the park with nothing but time on my hands and strangers all around me, the real challenge begins.

05/23/00

Well it took long enough to get here! The time is about 12:00 noon. I have never been so relieved in my life to be at a destination than I am right now. I am presently in my room at the Ahwahnee Hotel in Yosemite Park, and now my days of actual vacation have dwindled to six, including today. The hotel here is gorgeous with its wooden beams on the inside and the native stone structure that makes up the exterior. I walked through the sitting room, and it has to be one of the most beautiful in the world. Just staying here for a few days will test my credit card limits, so I'll probably move somewhere else soon and save money.

There's a surprise view of the Valley as you come through the tunnel on Highway 41 that is incredible. All of the Ansel Adams pictures I've ever seen came rushing back to me with every turn of my head. As you exit the tunnel on Highway 41, the Yosemite Valley suddenly spreads out before you. I had to stop my car for a moment and take a few pictures from the spot they call either Tunnel View or Inspiration Point. The brochure I picked up says both. From the view at the entrance, I've already seen El Capitan, Half Dome, and Bridalveil Falls, now I just need to get out and walk around a little.

The clerk here at the hotel told me I could have a room inside or there were also cabins in the garden area out back, which were the same price. One look at the cabins and I was sold. They sit out in a woody area with a paved path leading to the hotel in one direction and a river in the other. I've pulled all of my stuff from the car and unpacked most of it. The cabin number here is 723, so I'm inviting the future to come find me. But first I'm going to the bathroom and then out for a short hike, without my notebook, to enjoy the rest of the day.

05/23/00

The time is 11:45 PM, and I'm in bed for the night. I've been flipping through the courtesy Bible from the dresser drawer for some light reading, and it's made me a little sleepy. Wouldn't it have been great to be one of the Gideons and travel the world going from hotel to motel delivering Bibles? It would have been great to make a living seeing all the wonderful parts of America, not to mention the rest of the world. Arriving at a crazy hotel in the middle of a large city one night, then the next night staying in a beautiful motel seated by a quiescent river tucked away in the countryside. Truck driver or Gideon Bible distributor? That would be a tough decision for me. Why is it that some people find their calling too late in life? I could bore you with all the little details of my day, but I'm sure you wouldn't want to hear them, but I'll still give a brief overview.

After my last journal entry, I was excited to finally be settled in and on vacation, so I changed clothes and hurried out the door of my cabin, not wanting to waste a moment's time sitting around. I grabbed a snack from the shop in the lobby and ate it on the way out of the hotel. When I reached the hotel entrance and looked out at the Yosemite Valley and all the possibilities that lay in front of me, I immediately became overwhelmed and didn't know where to go. Motivation is a wonderful thing, but when it comes to actually applying it, fear can take its place very fast. All alone, my insecurities suddenly overtook me, and I had no focus or direction. My stomach began to hurt from nerves, and so I turned around.

Walking back toward my cabin, I passed the back patio of the hotel that leads to the garden. There was an open seat on the porch where several elderly men were sitting. Feeling perplexed by my situation, I sat down. One of the men to my left must have noticed a troubled look on my face as I sat there staring out at the wilderness. He said, "How are things today, young man?" Slow to answer, I said, "A little overwhelming." He said "Overwhelmed in a place like this? That shouldn't happen." He kept talking, and I just sat looking at the scenery and found myself settling in to the gentle sound of his mantra-like voice giving me instructions on life. He said, "You've got to learn to slow down when it comes to nature, it's not like the city. There you run to get things done, but here running just makes things worse, confuses you, because there's nothing to get done." My stomach started feeling better just listening to him talk. Then he made me laugh a little. He said, "See those mountains? They don't care if you get on top of them today or if it's tomorrow, they've been waiting there for millions of years for you. A couple of days won't make a difference to them." I wanted to say something in order to be conversational, but he didn't need to hear me, what I needed was to hear him. Then he started saying something like, "Nature makes you deal with certain things that you don't want to face." Thinking at this point that he might know something that I didn't, I asked him, "What kind of things?" He said, "Having to deal with yourself." He kept talking and I started to daydream, like I do when I feel good about myself. I can't recall exactly what he said after that, but I seemed to absorb the ideas, almost as if what he said was subliminal. We sat there on the porch in almost a father and son relationship for about an hour as he continued to talk. Eventually the talking stopped, and we all sat there quietly for another ten to fifteen minutes.

The men on the porch decided to go eat. They asked me if I wanted to join them, but I declined. I thanked the one gentleman who inspired me, and he just pursed his lips in a wise, simple smile and nodded his head. I left the hotel and took a walk in the nearby meadows, and my stomach didn't hurt anymore.

05/24/00
It's 10:50 AM, and this morning I'm sitting up in bed wondering how many nights I should stay here at the Ahwahnee Hotel. I like the place a lot, but it's quite expensive.

You also have to factor in that there have been no attempts to contact me even though I've given my cabin number and everything. My check out time today is at 11:00 AM, and I just woke up, so at this point I'll have to stay here again tonight. This place is very nice, but a bit haughty.

Sure I'm on vacation, and I should relax and enjoy a nice stay in a nice place, but I have to remember to test the limits of this book because this may be my last attempt before giving up. And I would hate to go back home feeling like I hadn't tried everything possible.

Since I've only been here one day, and was out most of the day yesterday, I think I'll try another night or two. I'll go check out Yosemite Lodge after lunch to see what it looks like and maybe make a decision.

05/24/00
Well I decided to rent a bike for the day, because it cuts down on smog in the valley. After riding around today, I found out that this part of the valley I'm in, and all the lodging places around here, is only a minor part of this entire place. I got a map from an information center earlier that shows the entire park, and there is so much more here than this small plot of land. This is just the location where the tourists gather at and hang out with their kids.

Anyway, I rode over to Yosemite Lodge to see what that area had to offer. I arrived just after noon and parked the bike. After checking out some of the lodgings, I walked around the area behind the main office and found several places to eat, as well as a bar and a coffee shop. There was also a small outdoor theater behind the front office of the Lodge where some sort of play was going on, so I sat down to watch. After a while I figured out that it was a Shakespearean play, but I wasn't sure which one at first.

They performed out on the stage with hardly any aids except costumes and a couple of pieces of wood that became whatever they needed it to be. That's all they really needed. I figured out that the play was "The Comedy of Errors." When I arrived, it was more than half over, so I decided to sit down and watch 'til the end. They told us that another group would be performing "The Merchant of Venice" at 2:00 PM out by Yosemite Creek, so I decided to hang around and watch the second play. There was a cafeteria right beside the outdoor theater, along with other restaurants and shops, so I decided to eat something. Vacation and overeating seem to go well together.

After getting somewhat lost trying to find the location of the second play, I arrived at the clearing where the performance was taking place. I was amazed that the actors didn't have a stage of any type erected. "The Merchant of Venice" is one of my favorite plays, and, with just a few props, these actors did one of the best jobs I've seen. The performance was set back away from the Lodge a little, and the wonderful thing about this one was that they used the surroundings as part of the play. Trees, rocks, water, cliffs, foliage, everything was planned out ahead of time and choreographed to accommodate nature as the stage.

Something else interesting was how the actors exited into the crowd when they were off stage. There was no back stage, so they just left wherever necessary at that point in the scene and stayed out until their cue came up again.

There was this one girl in particular whom I became enamored with who played the part of Portia. As the play went on, she would exit the stage (though there was no stage) and move around the crowd finding her next point of entry and wait. Like all the other actors, her part would be over and, if there weren't any costume changes, she would exit and wait until her next entrance. A couple of times she came over to me and carried on a small conversation. The first time she did it, I thought it was part of the actors working the crowd or something. There was one time when five minutes or more passed before her next performance, and she sat down beside me, and we talked quietly. She had beautiful blonde hair and, even though I'm clumsy with conversation, I was never at a loss for words. Usually I get anxious when talking to new people, girls in particular, and worry about the next topic of conversation, but with her that never happened. We talked mostly about the play, and she asked if I had read it or seen it before. I said yes.

She seemed very intelligent, and it amazed me how she would be into her character while on stage, exit, and then carry on a casual conversation. Then, when her cue arrived, she would leave, be in character, and not miss a beat in her performance. You would think that it would distract from the play with her doing that, but it all had a lighthearted feel, kind of like the theater atmosphere in Shakespeare's time, I guess. The play was great, but meeting her was the highlight of my day.

It felt nice to talk to her. I've basically been alone since leaving Los Angeles. Who knows? Maybe she was just working the crowd and had no interest in me. I'm not going to get my hopes up because too many times guys mistake kindness for flirting, and I've done that a few times myself. After the play was over, I came back to the hotel and enjoyed a couple of hours sitting on the porch. In a way, I was hoping the old men would be sitting out there again, but they weren't. Anyway, after the second performance, I came back to cabin 723.

It was nice over there at Yosemite Lodge, everything was centrally located and the people were more my class, younger and not so much money. Maybe I'll wait 'til the day after tomorrow to find a different place to stay. Tomorrow, I plan on getting up and going somewhere that's scenic and away from the crowds. Even though I've been complaining about being lonely, I think it would be a good experiment for the journal to be isolated.

I haven't been doing so much logging entries or watching for signs as I have been whining and telling stories about my day, so I should make a genuine attempt tomorrow. If the future is still reading this book, then they're probably falling asleep at this point. Well, I'm getting so tired that I can't keep my eyes open, so I'd better stop writing and go to sleep. Good night.

5/25/00

I got up early today and decided to take a hike. After breakfast, I grabbed my backpack and headed out with no specific direction in mind. I've been walking most of the day and just now decided to write. I brought a couple of sandwiches with me and sat below Vernal Falls and had lunch. I've been pensive all day for some reason but in a good mood. Maybe the middle of nowhere is a bad place for a contact, but you never know. After eating lunch, I went a ways down from Vernal Falls and I'm now sitting by the Merced River. The scenery here is beautiful. The whole day has been amazing and warm. There is a bird in the tree behind me telling me all about his day. I just wish I could understand what he's saying because he sounds really happy about something. It's nice being up here alone. Earlier I sat and played my harmonica in the woods for about a half-hour. Just walking through the woods, all alone, playing music, it was very peaceful.

Wow, I like the weather here, but a gust of wind like that one drops the temperature about 15 degrees. Just getting in the shade takes off about 8 to 10 degrees by itself without the wind whistling through the mountains. I'm glad I brought a long sleeved shirt out here with me.

I didn't bring my watch, but it's getting close to the end of the day, and the temperature is dropping fast. Now if I just had my tent and a sleeping bag I would stay out here all night. I just hate going back to the hotel right now. Maybe tomorrow, if I still feel the same, I'll splurge and rent a tent and just go for it.

05/25/00

A change of scenery seemed appropriate and with the sun close to setting, I wanted to find an opportune spot to observe it from. If I'm not mistaken, the Sentinel Bridge is just ahead of me in the distance. With the mountains blocking the sunset, I should get a good silhouette effect from this area. Now some clouds are forming on the horizon and the mountains and the bridge are turning a dark blue color, as the sky becomes a beautiful color of orange.

There is nothing more beautiful than nature. The poem "Tintern Abbey," by William Wordsworth, just came to mind while looking at this scene. He describes nature in a way that is beyond my abilities to express. Now I understand exactly what he was talking about.

There's a purple and orange aura forming just above the mountains now, as the sun has completely set somewhere on the other side of those peaks. Wow! That was the most amazing shooting star that I have ever seen. It crossed the sky going south and covered two mountaintops with the trail that it left. I can still see a slight smoke trail from it even now. How beautiful.

I wish I had brought someone here with me now. I hate to have a moment like this go by and no one to share it with. But it's certainly better watching nature's beauty alone than with a person who can't appreciate it. Surrey never appreciated it.

I hear voices coming from the other side of the bridge. It looks like a group of people is crossing the bridge from the other side. It looks like there are three guys and a couple of girls. They seem to be having a good time. Oh, I think these are some of the players from the Shakespeare group. I think the girl who played Portia is one of them. Yes, I'm sure it is now. They must all go to the same school or something because they seem like pretty good friends.

Wow! The girl who played Portia was climbing on the bridge just now and fell into the creek. Good thing it's only a small bridge and not a long drop. She may have even hurt herself a little, but she's just laughing. It looks like she hit her shin on the edge of the bridge too. She and her friends are all laughing as they're helping her from the creek.

I always envied people who could laugh at their own misfortune. When I was younger, I couldn't do that, I viewed my own mistakes with contempt and felt stupid for letting it happen. Maybe I was too proud. If people, even friends, laughed at my embarrassment, it would make me angry. But now that I'm a little older, I've tried to learn the joy of mistakes. Because I think the only mistakes to regret are the ones you learn nothing from. Still, I wish I could get to know more people who were positive like that. Because you only come around once, I think, and the mistakes, as well as the good moments, are all a part of life. Obviously it's easier said than it is done. I'm sitting here talking about it but not practicing it.

05/25/00
Well, it's almost midnight, and I'm lying awake in bed, so I thought I would write a little. I'm still thinking about the girl on the bridge and that whole incident. I do wish I could be more like that. And why can't I? I can talk philosophy about it all day long, but for some reason I can't absorb it. Is it really so difficult to change who we are that I can sit here and know what needs to be done, but not do it? Why is it that we are our own worst teachers? No matter what we know to be right, it takes someone else telling us the same thing to help us change.

Well, I'm not going to sit here and whine. That's not what this book is about, and I apologize for all the nonsense entries. Sitting here all night and writing about it would make me satisfied. That's not what I need. Maybe I'll just hold it in and, as it festers, I'll be forced to deal with it and make it change. Good night.

05/25/00

I got up early today and decided to take a hike. After breakfast, I grabbed my backpack and headed out with no specific direction in mind. I've been walking most of the day and just now decided to write. I brought a couple of sandwiches with me and sat below Vernal Falls and had lunch. I've been pensive all day for some reason but in a good mood. Maybe the middle of nowhere is a bad place for a contact, but you never know. After eating lunch, I went a ways down from Vernal Falls and I'm now sitting by the Merced River. The scenery here is beautiful. The whole day has been amazing and warm. There is a bird in the tree behind me telling me all about his day. I just wish I could understand what he's saying because he sounds really happy about something. It's nice being up here alone. Earlier I sat and played my harmonica in the woods for about a half-hour. Just walking through the woods, all alone, playing music. It was very peaceful.

This Is Incredible!

I was writing just before the last paragraph when the wind blew my journal backwards several pages. Looking back at several journal entries I found a duplicate of what I was just talking about, the same date and everything. But I'm telling you that I didn't write it! It's my handwriting, I looked at that already, and the place and circumstances are exactly the same, so even if somebody took my journal and copied my handwriting, they couldn't copy what's happening right now. My head feels very swimmy. I'm going to stop writing and lie down here for just a moment.

The grass is very cool and comforting. I'm feeling a little better now, but this is really bothering me. I'm flipping back and forth here and it seems that in the duplicate writing I rambled on about the weather for a while, and there's another paragraph following the duplicate one.

That's it! I've got to get out of here. What I need to do is go to the location listed and see if the journal matches exactly to what happens. This could be amazing. I wish there were someone here. I feel like telling somebody about this. I need to go now and check the other location.

05/25/00

My heart is racing, but it looks as though I arrived ahead of the other entry's time. This is crazy. I ran over here because there was no time given for the entry, I left my watch in the room. The descriptions of the sun going down behind the mountains, the surroundings, and the (Illegible word) tell me that I might have arrived early. I seem to have recorded a shooting star that crossed to the left of the mountains behind the bridge. If that takes place then I'll have to believe that the entry is a repeat. You can't fake a shooting star.

My writing may be sloppy because I'm flipping back to the other entries to see the differences. I'm also writing and looking up at the same time. I'll take a break here until the sky matches the journal, or something takes place.

Now the sun is close to the position described in the entry, clouds are forming on the horizon. The sky is turning a purple hue just like it says. This is beautiful.

There it went! I can't believe it! The shooting star actually went by in the same spot that was described, and it left a smoke trail that stretched across half the sky!

What am I supposed to think? How would something like this happen? I know I'm supposed to be looking for this but I have to be honest I never really expected something to happen, not like this. Now this, this can't be a fluke, or a lapse of memory. Something is wrong. And I don't know how to handle it.

Wait, I hear the people coming to the bridge now. There are two girls and three guys. The light is getting dim now. I see no reason for the journal to be wrong from here on out either. The girl should be joking around on the bridge and then slip off into the creek. Good thing she doesn't get hurt or I might have to rescue her.

No! What if I do go rescue her? If I get over there before she falls and stop her, then that would mean time is changeable. My heart is racing right now, I'll have to stop writing and make a decision. I don't have much time.

05/26/00

The time is 2:00 AM Friday morning, and I'm in my hotel room. The world seems completely different to me right now than it did just a few hours ago. I feel like something has changed inside of me, or maybe that I've gained something that has been missing for a long, long time. There's newness to everything around me, and life has a limitless feeling to it. Boundaries that used to restrict my thinking and hold me back from taking action have vanished. A lot of my worries, concerns, and fears are just gone.

Let me backtrack and explain myself as best as possible. I'll start from where I left off and explain the details in linear order so you'll understand how I got to this point. At the bridge my heart was racing so fast, and my mind so confused, that I didn't quite know what I was doing until it was done. I put down my book and ran as fast as I could to the bridge where the girl and her friends were. As I reached the bridge, I could see the girl starting to slip off the edge and as soon as I got to her, I caught her arm. At the pace I was running toward the group, I think I startled them. Once I had the girl by the hand, I helped her back onto sure footing. The others must have been too startled to help me. My mind began to absorb what had happened, and I looked around at this group of people staring at me. In the silence, I felt the fear of possibly having changed time by my actions, and also the embarrassment of barging in on a group of strangers. They just looked at me and didn't say a word.

The quiet lasted too long, and all sound seemed to disappear from the surrounding nature. The faces in front of me seemed frozen and impassive. Fear gripped me as the absence of sound and motion gave rise to the thought that time had stopped for everyone except me. For a split second, I thought that I had made the wrong decision and that now all life would stop because of one small action, but then something happened. The girl laughed.

I can't remember if it was shock or excitement, but her laughter startled me. It was as if her voice was the first sound from a new creation, a new beginning, and it split the air with new life. As her voice went out through the valley, it seemed to stir nature back to life.

Then, the whole world awakened, and her friends began to laugh with her. Exhilaration shot through me as the realization of what I had done set in. The thoughts penetrated my brain for only a second, when she spoke. She said her name was Gina and formally put out her hand. I shook her hand and introduced myself. She said "You saved my life." I told her she probably wouldn't have hurt herself too badly. Surely she didn't think that I saved her life, but she was sincerely grateful. Before I knew it, I was introduced to all her friends, and we were talking about the incident.

They started asking me where I appeared from so suddenly, and how did I know she was going to fall? I avoided the questions, but they asked again. I told them I saw that her footing didn't look safe and ran over to help her, and I apologized for startling them. They thought it was funny that I would apologize for something like that. They were very open and wanted to know whom I had come on vacation with. When I told them that I had come to the park by myself, just to get away from Los Angeles, they couldn't believe it. They didn't understand how someone could come all this way and spend this much time alone. I mentioned that I was working on a book and needed some time away from the city. Gina said she understood. The others started asking questions about the book, but I told them I couldn't say anything until it was finished.

So the next thing I know I was invited to spend the evening with them at a bar in Curry Village. At first I declined even though I found myself wanting to go. When they asked me the second time, I questioned myself on what was holding me back. Besides, this was a different timeline that I had created, and not venturing down this new path would be absurd. So I accepted.

We started walking back together, but we eventually split up, because they were staying at the Ranger Club. In the short conversation we had, I found out that they were workers here in the Park and not actors. They told me to meet them later at the Terrace Bar in Curry Village, and then we split up.

After we separated, I was so overwhelmed at what had just happened that it wasn't 'til I reached the hotel, and noticed my backpack hurting my back, that I remembered leaving my book on the rocks by the water.

My mind was in a blur as I ran non-stop through the park just hoping the book wasn't gone. I searched for a short while and then found the book, exactly where I left it. I put it in my backpack and ran back to the hotel. Once I reached my room with the book, I wanted to write about the incident before I left to go out, but I ran out of time. I didn't want to rush writing down the details involved, so I waited.

We met at the Terrace Bar, and the group consisted of Robbie, Jeff, Mike, Karen, and Gina. I found out that Robbie, Jeff, and Mike are friends of Gina's from when she worked at the Garden Terrace at Yosemite Lodge. Karen and Gina are roommates.

The thought of being the outsider in a group of people that all know each other scared me, but I was surprised how comfortable they made me feel.

When we got to the bar, we all sat down and had drinks, but it didn't take long for Gina and I to be the only ones talking, everyone else wandered off and left us alone. I discovered that the two of us had almost the same opinions on philosophy, science, and literature. I wondered if at first she was just being agreeable with my conversation, but when she started enlightening me on some of the subjects I thought I knew pretty well, it shocked me. We knew the same authors and liked the same philosophy, and we obviously both knew Shakespeare.

At one point, after several beers, we held a contest to see who could quote the most Shakespearean sonnets. People probably thought we were nerds because when we started out it was a dire competition, which we both took seriously, but very quickly the whole event became comical. She would start a sonnet and, half way through, I would finish it for her. Then I would begin the next one, and she would stop me within the first sentence to quote the last two lines. We ended up just calling it a draw.

This might all seem pretty pathetic for a lot of people, but for me it was great. I believe knowing someone intimately means knowing who they are. Between the two of us, though, I think she knew more about me by the end of the night than I did about her. The details I got from her were sort of general. She's the youngest in her family. She has two brothers. She's from Montana, and her mom wasn't around anymore. I wondered where her mom was but didn't press the question. Her birthday is coming up on 06/03/00, and she's going to turn twenty-three. She's been here about a year and works as a hiking guide in the summer and does concessions in the winter; the acting thing is sporadic park entertainment. She wasn't a guide when she first arrived, but she learned the area quickly, so they've given her the job this summer.

But the questions she asked me were deeper. One question she asked was where I saw myself in five years. That seemed to really throw me for some reason. With all the thought of time and its consequences, I had not considered my own situation just five years from now. For some reason, all my life, I haven't really felt that the future is set for me, it feels empty, or maybe, being more optimistic, open. I've felt this heroic urge as if some great feat will present itself for me to accomplish, but maybe that's just one of my many delusions. Anyway, my answer to her question was pretty much what I just told you, with a little more detail, and she seemed very understanding. We drank too much and talked a lot, and when we finally looked up from our conversation the entire bar was empty. We sat there alone on the open-air terrace.

Everyone had left us, and we didn't even notice. For at least another hour, we sat there rolling from one conversation to another not caring about anything, just enjoying the moment. And time really did seem to stand still. Finally, we decided to call it a night, and I walked her back to her place. I dropped her off at the employees' cabin and told her good night. Even though we went our separate ways at the end of the night, I felt that our evening was very intimate, yet comfortable. And sitting here hours later, I'm wondering why I didn't try to kiss her. I was so caught up in the moment that it didn't even cross my mind. Maybe that's a good thing.

As far as the double entry goes, I'm stumped. I've been looking back at the first entries, before the phenomena, and I see an entry made before midnight, as I lay in bed. Right now the time is a little past 3:30 AM. This would mean that I'm awake three and a half hours later than the other entry. What does this change for me tomorrow? Will the same things happen tomorrow that would have had I not gone to the bridge or stayed up late tonight? I don't think so, but oddly enough I'm not worried about it. People make decisions every day in a split second with no thought of the long-term ramifications. Walking to the store instead of driving, choosing which CD to listen to, or watching television much later than normal. This can't be any different, can it?

The question about the jump in time and how the double entry got there is a mystery, but from reading the entry and remembering getting up this morning, I have a theory. Somehow there must have been a shift in time, and I repeated one day twice. But you would think that if this happened then all the evidence would have been erased. My memories, peoples actions, everything would have been sent back a day with no signs of having been there or done that before. But whatever it was that caused the shift in time, somehow erased all the evidence except for the journal's entry. The only thing I can come up with is that the proximity of the book to my body may have had something to do with it. Last night, I fell asleep with the book in the bed with me. I've never fallen asleep with the journal by my side until last night.

This isn't much of a theory, I know, but it's all I have to go on. From now on I'm keeping the book in my possession at all times day and night. Whether or not an incident like this has happened before, I'm not sure, but if it happens again I want it recorded. This will also ensure that the book stays with me so that no tricks are being played. But if someone wants to contact me in person, they can still reach me, at cabin number 723 at the Ahwahnee Hotel, because I'm still here.

05/26/00 10:30 AM
It's the morning after now, and the past thirty minutes have been spent reading the last couple of entries in disbelief. I woke up this morning very groggy and having forgotten about the entry. I remembered it in

the middle of stretching and nearly hurt myself scrambling for the book. It only took a short glance at this notebook to see that it wasn't some weird dream, but I'm still stunned.

Maybe it didn't happen. Maybe it's all delusions of grandeur just like the definition in my psychology textbook. And what if I am making all of this up in my head? Right now it all seems foggy anyway, but then again I was drinking a lot last night.

I know that Gina is real, and the double entry is still here, but I don't know what to make of it. What I am sure of is that I feel good about myself, and the fact that the book has worked. Other than that, I don't think I care how it happened. But it happened.

05/26/00 8:12 PM
Presently, I'm sitting in my room and I've already had quite a day, let me see what I need to write about. After that last entry, I got up out of bed and decided to go looking for Gina. I looked around a little, but didn't know if she was still at the Ranger Club or working. I searched throughout the Yosemite Lodge and the grounds, thinking maybe she was doing another play, but I couldn't find her anywhere. Obviously it was a bit late for breakfast, and she does have to work. I assumed she was busy, and so I ate alone.

After eating, I put my notebook, along with a sandwich, in my backpack and took a hike. I didn't have any particular destination in mind, but I wound up by the Mirror Lake area, which is a couple of miles away from the hotel. The path up Tenaya Creek was so calming that I didn't notice how far I had gone. I sat down in a meadow and had my sandwich and watched the sun make the long shadows longer as it moved across the sky. The mountains seemed to gain depth as the sunlight cut into the crevasses and exposed the small valleys hidden inside.

All the troubles I've had at work and with this book seemed juvenile and distant today. Maybe it's the clean air or just being away from the worn-out duties of life that's changed my attitude, or maybe the satisfaction of achieving a milestone with this book. Then there's the possibility that it comes from having met someone that I can communicate with, and who sees things the way I do. I have been thinking a lot about her today, and that bothers me a little, but it makes me feel good too. I'm so used to being alone that feeling the slightest bit of emotional attachment frightens me. My fear has always been that once I find a girl I connect with, how could I ever part from her? The answer is that I wouldn't want to. But what if she doesn't feel as strongly about me? Is the remainder of my life spent wishing we had stayed together? Does the regret ever go away? I can't imagine how that old man William from the restaurant must feel. He still remembers and talks about Margaret as if it happened yesterday.

This could be the reason I'm alone a lot, because I'm afraid to let go and take the chance of being hurt. Too much of the time I worry about what the outcome of the relationship will be, instead of being in the moment and making it worth while.

Here again the book is a good analogy: I'm worried too much about tomorrow and the consequences it brings instead of enjoying the glories of today. I'm always looking to the past or the future and not recognizing today's possibilities. This has always been a shortcoming of mine.

I know I'm making a lot out of this because I just met the girl yesterday, and, yes, I have had a lonely few days leading up to this, so maybe I'm vulnerable. And yes, I over-analyze things, that's why I'm writing this overly analytical book, but I assume most people think about this stuff after meeting someone they feel attracted to, don't they?

Anyway, when I arrived back at the hotel, the time was about 6:00 PM, and I became a little worried about Gina, but didn't know where to find her.

After looking a while longer and not seeing her or even her friends from the bridge, I gave up. The first thing that came to mind was that she had gone home and said nothing to me, which seemed odd but not impossible. Then an even greater worry hit me and made me feel ill.

Just when my sanity feels solid and peaceful and my problems seem to ease a bit, I remember this book and its twisted possibilities. What if I changed something the other night that altered time? The incident at the bridge is what I'm referring to. Might my actions at the bridge have changed something unseen in a dramatic way? Without having any contact with people in Yosemite, except for Gina and her friends, a lot could have changed around me and I wouldn't know it. People, their characters, and how their personalities might now be different. Not to mention that I haven't watched television since I arrived. If things did change, maybe it's affecting more than just my surroundings. Maybe the effects go outside the confines of this park as well.

You see how quickly and to how great a degree I get caught up in this. I wish there were someone here I could talk to. Writing in the journal for therapy just isn't working anymore.

05/27/00

Yesterday, after my last entry, I stayed in my room the rest of the day. The only venture outside was for food and to check the surroundings for any of the group from the other day. The time is 11:00 AM, and I've just been sitting around this morning looking through the Los Angeles Times I picked up from downstairs. What I gather from reading the paper is that the world appears unaltered in spite of me.

The thoughts I was having yesterday about this stupid book altering time and life on earth seem insane. Probably the best thing for me to do right now is get out of this room and meet some people on my own. If nothing else, I've learned that all it takes is breaking free from myself long enough to take a chance at life, to do something that goes against that voice in my head that says "be safe, don't get out of your element." Once again, the voice of my childhood pastor comes back to me with one of his most memorable phrases. "Insanity is doing the same thing every day and expecting a change."

I can't predict tomorrow, and it may not be written down in my book, this time, for me to glance at and change the parts that I find unsuitable, but I can still change my destiny before it comes. The question I should ask myself is, "what can I do today that would make tomorrow different?" Building something that wasn't there or destroying something that was. Anything except sitting passively by and watching others do it.

05/27/00

After my last entry, I left the room and went to the lobby in the hotel, and there I sat trying to understand the mysteries of life in general and what was happening to me in particular. I sat there staring at the people and the surroundings until I got hungry. I ate at the Ahwahnee Lounge Restaurant and lingered there a while afterwards, drinking coffee, until I noticed the old man sitting on the back porch. So I decided to go outside and talk with him again.

He was by himself this time, and when he saw me coming he smiled at me, then he pulled up a chair from the table and turned it around for me to sit in. As I sat down he asked me how the pace was going? I told him he was right, it is hard dealing with yourself out here. He said something like, "They did it many millennia before we came along, and without all the technology. It takes practice. Don't try to do it all at once, tomorrow's another day." I wanted to tell him that for me tomorrow might just wind up being yesterday, but I didn't. Knowing that I had to be back at work on Monday, I told him my time was running out because tomorrow was all I had left. "Why only one day left?" he asked. I told him that I had to be back at work. He acted stunned, looked away, and then asked me, "Who's making you do that?" Then I became stunned, looked away, and thought about the odd question. I didn't really know what to say. After careful contemplation, I said, "Modern life." He looked at me and laughed.

"Well, I'd get away from that as quickly as possible if I were you." I wasn't sure how to get away from modern life? So I asked him that same question, and he said, "That's up to you, but I wouldn't let anything or anyone keep me where I didn't want to be." What I seemed to be missing lately wasn't as much an ear to hear my problems, but a wise voice to guide me. And he was right. I didn't have to work in L.A.. I could move, find another job, work here in Yosemite if I really wanted to. It was all an open book.

I left the hotel and took a walk alone in the nearby meadows. I wanted to just keep walking and not turn around. What would be so bad about that? The question came back to me, "Where will you be five years from now?" My chest started to ache. I was tired of the city, and I wasn't happy with my job. The hours were hard and the pay was low, and I couldn't figure out why I was still living in Los Angeles anymore. There's nothing to go back to there except bland existence. Right now I'm just living to make money in order to keep living. I can do that anywhere.

Sometimes I wish I could travel back in time to the era that those old men on the porch were from. Was it really better in the "old days," though? This man on the porch seemed to look right through me and to see my entire life. William, whom I met at the restaurant on the way here, seemed very wise and fulfilled despite all his heartaches, or maybe it's because of them. I don't know anymore.

I don't have to make a decision today anyway.

Great! I forgot to get the old man's name again.

05/28/00 9:00 AM

It's now Sunday the 28th. Basically, I can see no reason for me to be here any longer, especially since I have to be at work tomorrow. This vacation has helped me tremendously. I seem to have found myself, I've had a wonderful trip in spite of the troubles getting here, and I've experienced some things that I absolutely can't explain. It's been a nice stay, and besides, I got to repeat one day twice out of the deal. How many people can say they did that on vacation?

Work starts back for me tomorrow, and it will take me driving all day today just to get back, as long as everything goes trouble-free. As much as I want to take the old man's advice, I still have to be realistic. He's probably living his retirement and can say all he wants now. Maybe I'll be more like him when I'm retired.

I took one last trip over to Gina's place this morning and found no one there. I don't know what happened, but I wish I could have told her goodbye and thanked her for giving me inspiration to change things.

Well, it seems that my book may not be finished at this point. The repeated day baffles me. If someone wanted to contact me then they could have reached me by coming to my room. Did they try some other way? I can't explain it. Maybe I'll see a psychiatrist when I get home.

It's been very fun all in all. I need to continue my experiments when I get home. If a day can be repeated here then maybe something grander can be done elsewhere. I feel refreshed and renewed. No matter what the outcome...huh, someone's knocking on my door.

That was a strange surprise. Gina just showed up at my door and asked me to go to breakfast with her. I told her I would meet her in 30 minutes. I still want to finish what I was writing, but I'll do it when I get back.

05/28/00 11:00AM

I didn't expect to see Gina again. She told me she was needed at the Visitor Center near Tuolumne Meadows entrance, about 50 miles away, and spent the night there. She wanted to contact me before she left but had to go so early that she was afraid of waking me up. She seemed glad that I was still here, so that's a good sign.

When I told her that I had to be back at work tomorrow, she seemed disappointed. As sadistic as it seems, I enjoy the idea of her missing me. But now that Gina is here, I thought I could stay a little longer and get to know her a little better. So after eating, I came back to my room and called work to ask Allen if he could cover for me until Thursday the 1st. He said he could, and the management reluctantly OK'd it.

Since I'm staying in the Park a little longer, I'm going to move to Yosemite Lodge for the rest of the time. Anyway, Gina and I are supposed to meet up in about two hours and go hiking, so I'd better get a new room before I have to pay for another night here.

05/29/00 12:52 AM

From all I've gathered from the employees here at the park, this is the best time of the year to view the waterfalls because of the snowmelt. Now I believe them. Gina and I decided to walk over and see Yosemite Falls close up, which for some reason I hadn't done 'til today. There is a beautiful wooded trail leading up to the area. You can see the falls from several points in the park, but up close is a completely different experience. Yosemite Falls is actually three separate falls coming down an almost 2,500 foot drop. To see the water cascading off of that gigantic mountain in a torrent almost took my breath away. The sound of water rushing to the ground thrilled me so much that I decided to take Gina up close to the falls and get wet from the mist despite the chill in the air.

I think a connection began to build between the two of us as the day went on. She has this ability to free me from myself when I'm around her. I've heard people talk about feelings like this, but I thought they were just being ignorantly romantic or melodramatic. I guess I'm one of them now. I'm not saying it's love, but it feels like, well I don't know a word to describe it. The only way I can express it, at the risk of sounding silly, is that it feels like home.

I wanted to thank her for helping me break free at the bridge the other day, but that would've involved telling her the details, and I couldn't tell her the details. Later, we sat in the gardens outside the Ahwahnee Hotel, watching the sun set behind the mountains. We came back to Yosemite Lodge at around 8:30 PM. Hot chocolate sounded good to us after being out in the night air, so we went to the Mountain Room Bar, which was the only place still open, to see if they had anything there. The restaurant was too full and too loud so we decided to go to her place, because she had some instant chocolate. We went to her room and started to warm up and talk.

Our conversation went on for hours, about life and what it means, then rolling through philosophy, religion, school, travel, and somehow ending up with the Aborigines in Australia. Even when our views differed slightly, we still found a truth from the other that we hadn't seen before.

Oddly enough, I wasn't thinking about sex much, and I don't think she was either. We were so completely absorbed in the moment, and each other, that it was 11:00 PM when we noticed the time.

I didn't want to leave without making plans for tomorrow. The scene at the bridge came into my head, and I thought about the consequences of waiting too long and letting a moment pass me by forever, so without hesitation I said, "we should go camping tomorrow." It came out of my mouth before I knew what I had said, and I could feel the warmth of embarrassment begin to fill my face from the thought of rejection. She was excited about the idea but, unfortunately, she had to work tomorrow. I keep forgetting about her job because she seems to have a lot of freedom here.

Even though her excuse was legitimate, I still felt a sting of rejection. Quickly though, she suggested that we go Tuesday night instead because Wednesday was her day off, so we made it a date. Feeling exhilarated from making a bold decision and having it accepted, I decided to take a short walk before going back to Yosemite Lodge. The night air felt great.

Never in my life would I have had the where-with-all to express my opinion so boldly had it not been for the bridge. The idea of spending the night with her alone in the woods gave me butterflies at first, but it felt good. Decisions have always given me trouble in the past, but not anymore. From now on, I will consider them a challenge.

Good night.

05/29/00
Well, while Gina is working today, I really don't know what I'll do. The time is 8:05 AM, and I have the entire day ahead of me. I'm showered and dressed, so now I just need to decide what to conquer.

You know what's strange? Since arriving here at the park my watch has been off. I thought about mentioning it earlier, but kept getting distracted. I know that isn't the strangest thing you've ever heard, but what's weird is that every day I've put it on, or noticed it in the morning, I've had to adjust the time setting. Some days it's behind and other days it's ahead, which seems to rule out needing batteries, but when I compare my watch to other clocks there is always a discrepancy. One day it was so much off that I thought it had stopped, I think it was 5 hours behind. A part of me wonders if it's connected to the duplicate entry? Maybe the first thing I'll do this morning is look for a watch battery.

It's 11:04 AM, and I went to have my watch looked at. There was a guy down at one of the stores that said he could check it out if I gave him a day, but I told him I didn't want to hassle with it. My old one was getting beat up anyway, and I saw a watch I liked so I bought it. The new one went on my wrist and the old one went in my suitcase. If the watch was bad then that should stop the problem.

05/29/00 5:07 PM
Gina called a little while ago and invited me to go to a bar tonight just outside of the park. We're going with some people she works with to hang out, maybe play some pool, or whatever comes to mind. She says it's a fun place and that the people aren't pretentious, so it sounds like my kind of hangout. The Park employees get bored with the same old bars and restaurants here, so they like to go outside the Park for a little nightlife variety. I'm not drinking tonight, that way everyone else has a designated driver. Trust me you don't want any lapse of judgment while driving those curvy mountains roads.

I feel a little self-conscious about taking this book along with me because there's supposed to be a bunch of people, but I said I would keep it with me. I'll put it in my backpack with a couple of other things so it doesn't stand out. Besides, I shouldn't care
what people think about me, I've learned that if nothing else. I'd better finish getting ready so that I don't keep them waiting.

05/29/00
We're here at the bar, and I took a walk out to the car for a breather. It's almost midnight and I'm feeling a little under the weather for some reason, dizzy is actually what it is. Maybe it's because a couple of guys

were smoking in the back. I'll go inside in a minute. It's too noisy in there right now, and that just makes it worse.

05/30/00

I could hardly contain myself on the way back to the hotel because something strange has happened again. Shortly after I wrote the last entry, I went back inside the bar. I felt better, so I sat down beside Gina, where she was talking to some co-workers at a semi-circular booth. They were all drinking and talking, so I tried to stay quiet and just listen.

As I sat there, I started to feel dizzy again, and I thought it was from being in a stuffy room. Then I felt my head begin to sway and people's voices became muted as the vertigo overwhelmed me. Feeling like I was losing touch with my surroundings, I became unstable and grabbed hold of Gina's arm. She turned and looked at me, and I could tell she knew something was wrong. But that was just the beginning.

When I gripped her arm to stabilize myself, I felt her arm grow firm as she gave me an intense stare. For a moment, I thought it was the expression on my face that had startled her and made her stiffen up. She didn't move and her gaze didn't stop as I held onto her arm to keep from falling off the bench. When the noise in the bar became quiet, I thought I was going to faint, so I closed my eyes. There was no sound, no movement, no feelings, and I thought I had fallen to the floor unconscious. Either I couldn't or didn't want to open my eyes for fear that the sickness would come back. I don't know how much time had passed, but it seemed an eternity until I opened my eyes again.

When I finally became aware of my consciousness, I was still sitting holding on to Gina's arm, but everything had stopped. Everyone around me was frozen, motionless in front of me like sculptures. Gina was the only one looking directly at me. I slowly scanned the room to gain some kind of understanding. Looking back at Gina, I tried to move her arm, but it was like iron. I wanted to talk, but I couldn't. Or maybe I was afraid to, thinking that the slightest noise might shatter everything in the room.

People playing pool, drinking, eating, laughing, were all halted in mid action. It wasn't until then that I became aware that I could, and was, moving. As my mind struggled to think and my heart barely pumped, I stood up from the bench and began to walk. The air seemed stale and thick. Movement was slow and uneasy. I looked back to see if anyone had noticed me leaving the booth, but everyone was still looking in the same direction as before. I walked up to the closest pool table and noticed that a ball had stopped half way into a pocket. A guy, sitting at a table to my left, was in the middle of pouring a beer from a pitcher into a glass, but nothing was gaining or losing liquid.

I wasn't sure what was happening? Did I cause this? How would it stop, or rather start again? A woman leaning across one of the pool tables entranced me. She was laughing and her eyes were squinted, and her teeth were perfect. I walked over to her and looked at her face up close. I touched her skin and it was like porcelain. Her smile intrigued me, and I touched her lips, and then her teeth. I tapped on them both and they felt the same. Then for no reason, I looked in her mouth. Intrigue and awe were the only emotions I felt, everything else was dull.

Regaining some of my sensibility, I turned and looked toward the booth where Gina was sitting and noticed lights outside the window, just above her head. That's when I realized the car headlights on the road were stopped as well. I didn't know what to think. I walked slowly toward the window wondering what to do, trying to accept what I was seeing. There were several lights stopped on the road, but were they really cars? Had they stopping to look inside at us, or were they frozen as well? How far had this effect reached? As I got closer to the window, and leaned over the booth next to Gina, I could see the outline of a car, and the position of it on the road. Then suddenly a shadow passed in front of the lights moving at a fast pace. I thought it was a person. As soon as the thought crossed my mind the car headlights moved.

The music hit my ears violently, and the laughter and voices nearly took my knees out from under me. I covered my ears as the sounds of the bar came back with a deafening force. Opening my eyes, with my ears still covered, I saw Gina looking up at me from the booth. She knew something had happened. It must have seemed like I was sitting beside her one second, and then standing up the next second. I looked at her friends but they were too drunk and preoccupied to have noticed, and so were the people in the booth to the left and to the right by the jukebox, and everywhere else, so it appeared. Gina looked up at me and made a simple motion for me to sit down beside her. I was frightened, and maybe she was too, but she didn't say anything. And I wasn't about to.

I sat there just as stunned by the noise and movement as I had been moments before about the motionless void. A couple of minutes must have passed before my mind regained composure. Gina was turned, listening to the people sitting across from her as if nothing had happened, and I didn't know what to make of it all. I didn't say a word but I must have looked sick. The dizziness was gone, but this time I felt as though I would vomit if I didn't get a hold of myself. In order to distract myself, I focused my attention on the guy and girl sitting across from Gina. So I sat there and became fixated on the guy's mouth, and then the girl's. They laughed and talked effortlessly. How could something so supple and fluid become so rigid? The thought made my mouth hurt, and I reached up and began rubbing the muscles on the sides of my jaws. This made me yawn, and Gina noticed.

She turned to me and asked if I felt all right. Afraid to talk, I just looked at her and shook my head "no." She told her friends we were going to go, and I found myself saying, "I don't feel too well," just so she wasn't to blame. Her friends talked it over and decided to leave with us.

The ride back was very strange. Impatience was killing me because I wanted to get back here and write everything down. The two in the back seat talked all the way back, but Gina and I stayed quiet.

When I dropped Gina off, she asked me if I was going to be ok, and I told her I was. She was very concerned and said to let her know if I needed anything. She gave me her number, and then she kissed me and thanked me for going with her. That, I think, truly woke me out of my stupor. Believe it or not, her kiss was all I could think about while driving back to my place. It's probably the only thing keeping me from going loony right now.

The time is 3:21 AM, and I still don't know what to make of it all, the kiss as well as the incident.

05/30/00 10:08 AM

It's daylight now, and I don't know what happened last night. This is the second blatant phenomenon to occur since I arrived. What should I make of it? Should I ask Gina what she experienced? If there's no one to back up my experience, then I go between believing that it was real, and questioning my mental condition. There has to be a way to investigate this without mentioning it to Gina. I have to make some decisions.

The solution is to rule out the idea that it's a mental issue and start searching for tangible answers. But how do I go about that? How would I know if others experienced the same anomaly as I did? If time stopped, then there would be no clues or witnesses that it happened. Everything would have stopped with it, people, and events, even clocks. Wait! What about my watch! One thing I can do is check my new watch against the one in the suitcase. I haven't touched my old watch since I put it in with the luggage, so I don't know what time it says. Let me check.

The watch I bought two days ago, that I had on my arm last night, says the time is 11:38 AM, but the old one I put in the suitcase reads 10:18 AM. One of the two is wrong. The one watch is brand new, so it should be keeping good time. The time on the alarm clock agrees with my old watch, so that means my new watch is now having time problems. If all other clocks in the hotel match the one that was in my suitcase, then that means the watch I'm wearing is off by an hour and twenty minutes. Even if the incident at the bar actually did take place, it couldn't have taken an hour and twenty minutes. I know that Gina had her watch on last night, and if it differs from mine, then I will know something affected me and not other people. I'll have to get serious about this now. First, I need to check several other clocks in the hotel, as well as Gina's watch. Then I'll reset this one and take it off my arm to see what happens.

05/30/00

The time is 3:30 PM, according to the room's alarm clock. I guess I need to put my book, along with some necessities, in my backpack, then I need to shower. Gina is supposed to meet me here at 4:30 PM to go hiking to the campsite, about two miles on the other side of the Ahwahnee Hotel. We're getting a late start because she was working today, but she knows the area well. Gina said that very few people know about this location, and even though it's not in the untamed wilderness it should still be secluded. The top of El Capitan is where I wanted to go, but she said it takes two days to camp out and enjoy the scenery, so we're going somewhere closer. Gina has all of the camping gear we need, so I don't have to do much except show up. Seeing how we'll be together most of the time, I'm not sure if I'll get away to do any writing. She knows I'm here to write a book, though, so I'll just tell her I need a little time by myself.

I have to be honest, I'm a little nervous about this trip because I'm not sure what to expect. She seemed to have no hesitation about going camping with me. I feel like I'm a kid on his first date again. I can't help but think I'll do something embarrassing because I'm so nervous. What's going on in her mind? A better question is what is she expecting? She did kiss me.

Damn it, I've got to stop this. There I go again looking to the future and trying to predict it, at least I caught myself this time. If I sit here worrying about the end result before it even begins, then I could make myself sick and not be able to go. All I need to think about at this point is getting my stuff together and being ready when she gets here, that's all. That makes me feel better already.

05/30/00

It took us a little while to hike to the site, and the sun went down on us before we got here, but now we've set up the tent and lit a lantern. Gina brought this black tube with us that they call a "Bear-box" or something like that. You put your food in it so bears don't smell it and attack you. I didn't know that. Twice, I've taken sandwiches out in the woods without thinking about bears attacking. Anyway, I decided to get away and make an entry, so I'm sitting on a large boulder writing by the light of a flashlight, keeping one eye out for bears.

Gina seems to be very understanding about my writing. I told her I have to get away and write whenever an idea comes to mind. She said she's the same way about writing, and mentioned that she had a journal. Earlier I stuck my watch in my backpack so that Gina wouldn't see it. A little while ago I asked her what time it was, and she replied that, "time doesn't matter out here" and showed me her bare arm. She must have left her watch back in her room. I'll just wait 'til tomorrow and check her watch while she's not looking. It's hard not to be anxious now that two of these distortions have affected me.

But she's right. I can't worry about time while I'm out here. It's just her and me in this gorgeous place, and I'll regret not taking advantage of it if I spend the entire time investigating. It's amazing out here. I can see the stars clearer than I've ever seen them before. I guess I should get off this boulder and head back to camp. Hopefully I won't meet any bears along the way.

05/31/00

Well it's a very beautiful morning. Gina is still asleep, and it's early. I can't sleep late while camping, I don't know why. Maybe it's the birds or the fresh air, or even the break of dawn creeping under my eyelids, but, whatever the reason, it seemed to be a good time to sneak away and write in private.

Last night, after my entry, I walked back to where the camp was, and Gina had some hot chocolate already made. So I sat beside her, and we sipped hot chocolate while we talked. I was nervous, so I decided to ask her some questions. I wanted to know more about her, and at the same time see what she remembered from the other night. I started by asking about the journal she'd mentioned writing, and it seemed like the gates opened up, and we started talking. Soon I found out that I didn't know as much about her as I had assumed.

She began by telling me her present journal is the eighteenth book in an almost continual account of her life since she was the age of six. Her dad encouraged her to write at a young age. He saw how much she liked books, so for her sixth birthday he bought her the first journal. He later regretted that decision when she was ready to go to college and her interest in writing had grown. What her father wanted was for one of his children to follow in his field, which was Engineering, but her two brothers were poor in math skills and had already finished college with other degrees. She proceeded to follow writing and majored in English. Her father's persistence for her to be an Engineer prevailed anyway, and she ended up getting a degree in Engineering as well. Gina says she was under pressure not to disappoint her father, but also that mathematics and Engineering came natural to her. Gina went on to say how she would hate to be stuck doing anything else in the world except what she wanted. Working in Engineering was so stale that it would have been the death of her, she admitted, because it had no creativity and no life. Why, I asked her, would a person with a double major be working here in a National Park?

For a minute, she didn't say anything and just looked down at the dirt. It made me feel a little guilty for asking her the question. Maybe there were family issues involved, or something else personal. Or maybe she was just doing like the old man at the hotel suggested, not doing anything she didn't want to. As soon as I was about to apologize for being nosey, she let out a sigh and looked up at me. Just before she spoke, the look on her face could have melted my soul. It's as if she were hiding something that was hurting her. I don't know if she came to Yosemite running away from something or running to something, but her answer didn't satisfy me.

She said that half the reason she's here is to find herself, and the other half was just like me, she wanted to get away and continue her writing. She tried to divert the questions and asked me when she could purchase a copy of my book. I tried to diffuse the uneasiness and told her, "If you're lucky, never."

She laughed, and before I knew what was going on, she had rested her head on my shoulder. Without hesitation, I put my arm around her, and I think I fell in love. At that point, I had no interest in asking about the other night at the bar.

After we ate, I pulled out our sleeping bags and laid them on the ground outside the tent. The air wasn't too cold and the sky was clear, so we just sat back and star gazed. The conversation slowed down as we began talking about the constellation Orion and The Big Dipper and watched a couple of shooting stars cross the sky.

With the lights all out, and the night pitch black, I asked her what she thought the future would be like. We both exchanged wild stories about what we expected it to be and then somewhere in the conversation we fell asleep.

The sun's up a little higher now, and she might be waking up soon. So I'll head back to the campsite before she gets up and thinks a bear has eaten me. This place is so beautiful. Just thinking of going back to Los Angeles and the mundane job is killing me. I'm sure I can't stay here, but I don't want to go back there. I have to leave today if I'm going to make it to work tomorrow.

05/31/00

Gina and I came back from camping about 1:00 PM, and I've been pondering what to do with my life. What would happen if I didn't go to work tomorrow? It's already so late that I wouldn't get home 'til around midnight if I left now. Maybe, deep down, I'm resisting without saying so. Gina knows I'm supposed to leave, and she told me to call her if I leave tonight, so she could say goodbye. She didn't say much on the hike back, except that she understood I had to leave, and that she would miss me. We agreed to keep in contact, but that long distance thing doesn't ever work.

Where do I go from here? There's the old man on the back patio with his words of wisdom, then there's William at the restaurant who's story is still on my mind, and it seems on every side I have these signs telling me not to regret life, and to make a move contrary to what my inner voices tell me. How do I know what's right? What would I do if I stayed? This book is the only thing solid I have in life, and that's not saying much. Would the regret of staying here, and failing, outweigh the regret of going back to L.A.?

05/31/00

It seems things are about to change for me. I've taken on the task of directing my life instead of letting it pull me around. The time is 8:32 PM, and I'm about to meet up with Gina. I called and asked her to meet me tonight at the Mountain Room Bar at 9:00 PM, and she agreed.

I think I'm going to tell her about the book and anything else she wants to know about me. The thought of leaving her is hurting so bad I can't think straight. Maybe this is just a childish feeling I'm having and she doesn't feel the same way, but that's what I'm about to rule out.

I don't want to end up like William holding on to the past for the rest of my life, or even worse, regretting not knowing what might have happened because I didn't ask. The simplest act can change a person's life; I can see that now. It's possible to change our future with the smallest question, and that's what I hope happens tonight. Not marriage, not love forever, but at this point just finding a way to be together a while longer. To make sure that we don't regret not trying, that's all. I'll work here in the park if that's what it takes. We'll move to Montana if she wants to be closer to her dad. We'll move to Japan if she wants to learn a new language.

Work wants me back by tomorrow, and the way I see it, I can't go back to work now or else everything is in vain. Actually, I called work already and told them I needed more time. They said "no," so I had to quit. I don't care anymore. All I know is, whether Gina feels the same about me or not, I've committed myself to change, and it's all in the hands of fate.

05/31/00
The time is two minutes 'til 10:00 PM, and the Mountain Room Bar is closing. Gina was supposed to meet me here at 9:00 PM, but she still hasn't shown up. At 9:15, I called her place but no one answered. They'll be asking me to leave pretty soon. I'm worried about her. I think I'll check her room.

05/31/00
It's nearly midnight, and I couldn't find Gina in her room. And neither Karen, Gina's roommate, nor her neighbors have seen her. Karen said she would help me search for her and even offered to drive me around. I just said "no" and walked away. She invited me inside to sit and wait for her, but I just kept walking. Now I'm sitting in the lobby of the Lodge, and I don't know what else to do. I can't believe that she wouldn't show up.

05/31/00
I just came up to my room and found a letter from Gina under my door. I can't explain it. I can only copy it into my journal.

Dear Jason,

Let me begin by saying I'm sorry for not showing up tonight. I hope you didn't get too worried about me before finding this letter. There are some things we need to talk about, and hopefully tomorrow I can give you more details.

I had to meet some people tonight about a very important decision, one that concerns you. This isn't easy, and the only way I can explain it is just to come out and say it.

I know about your book. I know everything about you and why you're here. Actually, that's not true, I don't know everything about you, I only thought I did until we met on the bridge. Please don't be upset with me for telling you all of this in a letter. I wanted to tell you personally, but it wasn't up to me. Since I first realized who you were, I wanted to tell you about this, but it took everything I had not to. This may all sound like nonsense right now, but please believe me. There have been many discussions and calculations to get to this point.

I'm sorry if this letter seems clinical, but I haven't much time. There are a couple of rules you must adhere to at this point; people's lives may be at stake. Whatever you do, you can't change any of the pages that have already been written in your journal. There could be dire consequences if anything is altered, even our experiments could be changed. Also, if you have to leave the park, please at least let me know first. I know you're supposed to be at work tomorrow, but I wish you wouldn't go.

Also, don't open the door for anyone you don't know, and don't go anywhere that's unnecessary. This sounds strange, I'm sure, but you're going to have to trust me. A lot of things must be going through your mind right now, but be assured that this is real, I'll give you proof.

We would like you to leave this time period for your own protection. I realize we can't make you do something you don't want to do, so the choice is ultimately yours alone. But if I have any influence over your decision, then I would ask that you please come back with me. Most of my life has been spent trying to understand who you were, but now I feel I truly know you. I wish I could have told you in person, but hopefully I'll get the chance.

There's so much in store that you can't even imagine, I can't wait to see your face if you say yes. Your decision has to be quick, though. I'm sorry, but our time window is closing.

One last thing, you can't bring your book with you. It has to stay. I can't tell you what to do with it, and I can't tell you how it's found. I'll explain later. Tonight I'll be at my place, so call me as soon as you read this. I'm worried. I want to know that you're all right.

There's a key to my door in the envelope. In case you have to leave the room for any reason, please come over. Anything I have is yours.

Love, Gina

06/01/00

I copied that note last night and immediately called Gina and told her I wanted to leave with her. I was very excited, and I'm still stunned. Not only have I left my job and the life I'm used to, but I seem to have proven a theory that might be the first of its kind.

Gina and I talked for hours last night, but it wasn't as much about the trip or even what I should expect, but more about us. We talked about how strong the attraction was the first day we met at "The Merchant of Venice." I told her I would start calling her Portia and that we defiantly had to visit Venice. It completely slipped my mind to talk to her about the incident at the bridge. I have so many questions left to ask her. The time is 8:30 AM, and I'm getting ready to go into town. Gina quits her job at the park after today. She wants me to come to her place and stay the night so we can leave tomorrow morning.

Last night I couldn't sleep and I couldn't write. All I could do was lie on the bed while my mind boiled with innumerable thoughts. It was as if I was dying. My life and my experiences kept washing over me. Feelings and sentiments kept pleading for me to stay here. Memories of my family back home and the life that I had put together kept bombarding me. It was a constant battle, and I almost decided not to go. Then I remembered all of the bad relationships I've had in my life, whether business or romantic, and how when I was finally rid of them I still felt a sense of remorse, much like I do now. That's how I saw it. Changing from any situation to another is emotional. Even the worst situations can be tolerated once you get accustomed to them. I don't want to be comfortable.

I'm not sure exactly where we'll be going, but Gina talks about going somewhere in the Tuolumne Meadows just East of here and so that's our destination. I'm going into town to withdraw the money from my savings account and also to put my book in a safety deposit box. My hope is that Calvin will take care of the journal for me. He's very resourceful and has a way of getting things done. Out of everyone I know, he has the ability to get the book to the right people. Gina said she couldn't tell me what to do with the book, so, to me, he seems the logical choice. And I won't tell him what to do with the book. That way it's like a double blind psychology test.

06/01/00
It would be faster and seem wiser to mail the book, but I can't trust it to go safely through the mail. This book means too much to me right now. With a safety deposit box, I know he'll get it. And if he doesn't, then some bank official in the future will and, who knows, maybe that's how it's found. If Gina and her people have my book, or some form of it, then it doesn't matter what I do. It all works out, right?

I've just been to the bank and withdrawn money and set up a safe deposit box for the book. Now I'm sitting outside the post office ready to write the letter and ask Calvin to come all the way to California and pick up the book.

06/01/00
This is it. I'm in the post office now about to mail the letter. I decided to bring the book with me just so I can make every possible entry before letting it go. I've become very attached to it. In the future, I'll have to pick up another journal like this one.

The letter isn't long and so quoting it will be a fit ending to my book.

06/01/00

Dear Calvin,

This may sound very strange from your point of view but please read this letter carefully, and with a sincere trust in my sanity. I need your help. You should receive this letter about four days from today's date. If you haven't heard from me by now then consider this letter our last communication. I need you to come to California and get my notebook.

The book is located in a safe deposit box at _____Bank in _____ California. I can't tell you what to do with the book; you will have to decide what's best. Inside the safe deposit box you will also find some money to use at your discretion. I assume you've already found the key to the deposit box taped down inside the envelope.

I know it's a lot to ask, and I'm sorry that I can't be more specific, but I promise you will understand all of this when you read the notebook.

You are the only one I can trust. My future depends on you.

Jason Edmond

06/01/00
This is it. The letter is in the mail and out of my hands now. I'm back at the bank sitting on their plush sofa about to put the book in the deposit box.

Now it's painfully apparent how little I believed that this would happen. It all started as a silly idea in order to amuse myself, and now this. I just wanted to attempt something daring in a life full of complacency, never really thinking that it would come to anything.

What's ahead for me? Should I eagerly accept what I'm about to do, or be concerned, like I had advised myself earlier in the journal? No, I shouldn't worry, and I won't.

Wow, I've just realized that you are actually sitting out there somewhere reading this book. For the first time, I know that you're reading what I'm writing. How long has it been? What year is it? I'm here in 06/01/00, where are you? What's your name? Do I bore you? Were you forced to read this? Oh, I truly hope not.

I had to laugh out loud just then, and several people in the bank looked over at me. Who cares, though? Don't care too much about things, that's my advice to you. It's not...

I'm sorry, the TV is on in front of me and the news just reported that someone fell off one of the falls at Yosemite. That's horrible. They just went to a commercial. I'll wait for just a minute and check it out. That looked like Gina's yellow jacket!

06/01/00

I've just reentered the park. Am writing while driving. Forgotten how far this drive was. I hope I'm wrong. It looked like her. It was at a distance. (Illegible sentence) Probably driving (Illegible)...not thinking straight. My park admission expired. Had to renew fee to get in. Need gas.

I've stopped now, I'm filling up at Wawona. I hope that wasn't her. My head is beginning to hurt. Let it be someone else. Maybe her roommate borrowed her jacket. No, I don't want it to be her either, not anybody. I need to get out of here. I'm not going to wait for the car to fill up.

06/01/00

Here now at the medical center in Yosemite Valley where they take injured people. It was Gina who fell. They think she was giving some type of hiking tour when she slipped and fell. I wanted to see her, but they told me I couldn't because I wasn't related. She is here, and they told me she wasn't doing well. How could this happen? They wouldn't give me any details. One of Gina's co-workers is here and she said they were going to mediflight her to Doctor's Medical Center in Modesto as soon as they stabilize her. I couldn't just sit around any longer, I'm walking around outside because I'm shaking too much.

What was she doing up there on the falls trail? We were supposed to meet at her place in just a few hours. She wasn't supposed to be giving a tour today. How could she have fallen? If only there were something I could do to change things. Somewhere in the back of my mind I'm hoping, … Why can't someone in the future change the way things have gone? If someone is reading this that can help change things… Something is obviously happening to me. If nothing else then let me skip backward to yesterday again, or even earlier this morning, to change things. I'll do it. Take me back as far as you need, just as long as I can still remember what to do when I get there.

You've been playing with me since I arrived here, so why can't you do something now when I need it? Are you doing this on purpose? Is anyone really reading this who could help me? Are you seeing how far you can push me? If you have my book, then you can see what I'm writing.

I feel like an idiot for even writing that last paragraph.

06/01/00
The doctors came in and told us that Gina died at 5:14 PM, while they were trying to stabilize her for transport. There shouldn't have been a double entry. There shouldn't have been that double entry and then it wouldn't have happened. Why did I interfere? It was selfish. Why did I even start this stupid, idiotic... I met her on the bridge. That's what started it all. Then she said it herself in the letter. I want to know who caused the double entry. That's what brought us together. What an idiot I am. Someone in the future must know about this. Why aren't they talking to me? If you're reading this then you've got to be able to fix it? What kind of person, what malevolent creature would sit by and allow this to happen? I can't take anymore of this!

This place isn't beautiful anymore.

06/01/00
I don't know where I am. I'm just walking. I don't know what time it is, and I don't care. Something went wrong. No one is reading this. No one is reading any of this. She must have lied to me about everything. Why would she lie? She was so beautiful, she would smile at me and nothing else mattered. Strange how loud it sounds out here. I can hear everything. "How weary, stale, and flat seem to me the uses of this world! Wish God had not fixed his canon against self-slaughter." Now I know how Hamlet felt. If I could go back I would take her place. But I don't know where to go. I'm just standing here. In the middle of a bunch of trees not knowing what to do. I've been here for a while now. I don't know what to do. I could have lost everything except for her and that would be fine. I've never felt this lonely before. It's all because of this book. This book here in my hand that I won't let go of.

I want to throw it in the lake, but that's probably where someone finds it.

No, this isn't right. I've got to start thinking. I have to find an answer. Gina wouldn't lie to me. She gave me proof that she knew about the book. Someone has to be reading this, and there must be a way to contact them. But how did she know? Who was she talking with? Where would I look for them?

She was taking me somewhere, and I was going to meet them. She said she had a journal! If I can find that journal maybe she mentions a name, maybe the place she was taking me. If not, then I might find something in there to help me, anything. If I can get to the future, then they can get me to the past. And if I can make it to the past then I can change things. I'll have to find her journal before anyone else finds it. She gave me a key to her place.

06/01/00
Hope no one else has been here yet. I want to do this fast. There's no one walking around her place that I can see. It looks like no one's inside either. I'll go knock on the door, as if I'm coming to see her. If no one answers, then I'll go inside.

06/01/00
My heart never beat so fast in my life. My nerves are shot and I'm panting. I'm back in my room now, and I have Gina's journal with me. Part of me feels bad for having taken something from her room, especially her journal, but under any other circumstances I wouldn't have. I'm almost afraid to read it. My stomach feels nauseous.

There may be a few bad spots on these two pages and I apologize. I got sick and barely made it to the bathroom, but I wiped (Illegible phrase) as well as I could. I'll have to lie down for a few minutes and see if I can calm down some.

06/01/00
It's dark out. The time is 7:35 PM now. I didn't mean to fall asleep. I guess the stress… I'd almost forgotten. I just want to sleep and not

wake up. It hurts too much to think about it. I don't want to think. This room is very lonely. I'm shivering. Sorry if my writing is shaky.

Her book is sitting on the dresser. I can't get up to get it. I don't want to get up. I don't want to get it. I have to be honest; I don't want to continue feeling like this. How do I make it stop?

06/01/00
I wish the sun was up. It's 10:12 PM. As much as I feel like lying down again, I know that I can't make any progress if I don't push forward.

Her journal has a beautiful red cloth covering, unlike my black nylon mesh binder. There's no latch holding it together and no lock-and-key system to it. I guess that's just what I would expect a girl to have. She must not have been worried about anyone reading it. Well, I'll have to stop writing now if I'm going to read this.

06/01/00
It's been about an hour now, and I've only read about fifteen pages into her journal. I keep reading the same sentences over and over. Maybe I can concentrate better if I write what I'm reading. I'm going to copy parts of it into my book. Her entries started about a year ago. I'll write down her first entry and then skip forward so I can find some current information.

> Gina's journal 05/20/99
> I can't believe I'm here. I just bought this book an hour ago and I'm sitting by the Merced River feeling fuzzy from the trip.
>
> Everyone involved in the transition has been so very nice. As soon as my examination at Tuolumne Port was over I met Morgan, and he took me through orientation. It's funny. Back here they pronounce Tuolumne differently. Yosemite is spelled a little funny too, if you ask me.

Morgan is here to help me with adjustments, accommodations, and general questions about this time period. He also has the Link, so any messages will come through him. Basically I have about a year to get adjusted to my job and the environment before the real test comes. I'm so excited! My father still hates the idea. He's never satisfied. The time here is 3:14 p.m. My father gave me a watch for my birthday, this will be the first one he's missed. I hope he's not too upset with me. This adventure is the closest thing that we've both worked on since my science fair project in elementary.

Out of all the people in the world, I never thought I would be the one to come back here. I bet that's how people back in the 20th... that's funny, I forgot where I was for a minute, how the people in this century feel about space travel. If I make a verbal faux pas like that again it could get me in trouble.

Usually when I start a new journal, I write some predictions for myself, for when the journal's full. But this time it seems predictions are way too limited. Besides, if you want something to happen you have to make it happen.

06/01/00
Just skimming through Gina's journal I can see that I have to jump to the present in order to copy what I need to read.

Gina's journal 05/25/00
Yesterday was so nice. Karen and I put on another play near Yosemite Creek. "The Merchant of Venice" this time. And finally I got to play Portia! It was a nice day. We did the play at the amphitheater this time, despite the heat, and I just loved it. A lot of people showed up and most of them stayed 'til the end.

Karen introduced me to a guy she's been seeing who came out to watch us and I met a nice guy myself in the audience.

So, all in all, it was a good day. I really wish we were doing one more play before I leave. I love my friends here. And the air here is so nice and the people are so innocent. It's going to be very difficult leaving.

I reported to Morgan today just to keep him up to date. He could tell by the tone of my voice I was getting a little anxious about the coming weeks. He said I could be going home anywhere from one week to two months from now, depending on what happens. Either way the next few days will sure test me.

By now Jason has to be in the park, or soon will be. His only surviving journal entry from Yosemite takes place at Ahwahnee Hotel on 5-27-00. Just two days from now. Just thinking about it gives me this odd feeling of fear and euphoria. But my job is just to "observe and record," nothing else. The guidelines are simple. I can't intervene.

06/01/00

Right now I want to write on every page "don't send Gina." She says that the entry on 05/27/00 is the only one from Yosemite that survives. Maybe that's it. Wherever they find my journal it must be in such bad shape that only portions of it are intact. I could go back to the earlier pages and cross them out and write, "Don't send Gina" on all of them. But I can't. She said in her letter that there could be dire consequences if I change anything. I'll have to make a decision soon whether or not to go against that.

If only she'd told me where they found my journal, then I could wrap it in steel and put it there. Maybe one of her entries will tell me.

Gina's journal 05/26/00

Early today I called Tuolumne Port and spoke with Morgan. I reported that I came in contact with Jason last night at a bridge. He said that it should be all right, but when I told him the extent of the contact, he got concerned. He called it in, and everyone requested that I stay overnight at Tuolumne to avoid influencing Jason's entries tomorrow.

Morgan cleared the O.K. for me to take off work today and tomorrow.

I arrived here at Tuolumne about 10:00 a.m. The others have been pretty critical of me for interfering with Jason. I couldn't count the number of times I heard the phrase, "observe and record only." And they didn't seem to believe that he initiated the contact. Karen shouldn't have invited him to go out with us, but we were both excited when he told us his name. The Tuolumne group debated whether it would be best for me to return to the park or stay here and let him forget about meeting me. Using my often persuasive personality, I insisted that I return. Anything changed by my contact with him, I argued, has already been altered in the future. They didn't want to debate the ethics and theories of time travel with me, so they reluctantly conceded.

I'll be staying here overnight and then returning early on the morning of 5-28-00 so that his entries for 5-27-00 can be done without any interference from me.

I still don't know how he saw me and knew I was about to fall off the bridge. When I was in school studying the book, I always loved his first entry from 5-27 and thought it was the most inspirational entry. Not just because 5-27 had the last two surviving entry pages of the book, that's why the others liked it. I found it to be some of his most honest writing.

I really do understand everyone's concern, especially considering the 5-27 entries are the only ones that place him at Yosemite. In school there was the controversy over the one passage that read "I can't predict tomorrow, and it may not be written down in my book, this time, for me to glance at and change the parts that I find unsuitable, but I can still change my destiny before it comes." What did he mean when he said, "… written down in my book, this time?" In school the question was whether he had some sort

of early premonition or contact. Now being here on this end
I wonder if it had anything to do with me, or even worse,
rogue agents. No one here can be sure that others aren't
trying to contact him, or even kidnap him. In a way I'm
afraid to leave him alone while I'm gone. They did train me
and prepare me to protect him. But he should be safe, I
hope. He has to make the journal entry, so surely he'll be all
right.

06/02/00

It's morning now, about 1:00, and I'm finding it hard to believe what
I'm reading from her journal. The way she talks about me, it's like
she's known me forever. It's unsettling. When I met her, I had this
feeling, like we were suppose to be together. And from what I'm
reading, she may have felt the same thing a long time ago (or a long
time from now, depending on how you look at it).

My eyes are starting to blur from reading, and my head hurts. All this
is too much for me to think about right now. I'll just keep copying.

> Gina's journal 05/27/00
> Since I have to spend the rest of today at Tuolumne, I've
> decided to read a copy of Jason's journal and I've
> discovered what threw me off. At the bridge, Jason told us
> he was alone at Yosemite, but the 5-27 entry mentions
> checking the surroundings for "the group." If he had come
> alone, could "the group" be a tour group? One prevailing
> theory was that he met up with friends or family at the last
> minute. Now that I've been there, I shudder to think that he
> may have been looking for my group, the friends I was with
> on the bridge. I'm not at the Park now, and he might be
> looking for us, me. That wouldn't be good.
>
> Wait, if he were looking for my group when he wrote that,
> then I didn't change anything by being there. It's possible
> that he was writing about me back then, and he might be
> writing about me now? That entry was written before I was
> born, even before my grandfather was born. Could that one

reference, made in his journal, the one that has stumped teachers and professors for so many years, be about me?

Gina's journal 05/28/00 6:00 AM
We're about to leave for Yosemite Valley. Morgan will drive me back to the park. He hasn't said much to me about the contact. I didn't mention my theory about "the group," but I'm sure he's thought something similar. With my every move being relayed back to Base, they're probably calculating every possible scenario and timeline change imaginable. If their doing it right then they've come up with the same things I have, and then some. So I'm wondering why they're still sending me back. No, I know why they're sending me back, because deep down we're all scientists. As risky as another contact with Jason may be, their curiosity gets the best of them, and me. And since Jason's last surviving entry has already been made, I can't screw up anything, so why not?

There's Morgan at the door. I have to go.

Gina's journal 05/28/00 8:00 AM
I've arrived at Yosemite Valley and am back in my room. Morgan and I talked a lot on the way here. It seems that Base is deliberating whether or not to ask Jason to come back with us for his own safety. They seemed to be worried about rogue agents even more now.

But I know these guys. What they're really after is his journal. They want it complete and in their hands. All I want is for Jason to be safe, and for him to come back with me. I haven't said much about it to anyone, but I do have feelings for him. Concern, mostly, but something more than that too.

Morgan said that Base is proud of what I've done, and that they're glad they picked the right person for this job. Basically, they're trying to bloat my ego. At the risk of the

Base Camp commanders reading this later, I think they're full of crap. They want what they want, and that's pretty much it. If I can pull something good out of it for myself, then I'll do that.

I think I'll go over and see if I can find Jason now. It's early enough that maybe he's in his room.

Gina's journal 05/28/00 10:50 PM
Today was the most memorable day of my life. I found Jason in his room this morning, and we went and had some breakfast. It seems he was genuinely glad to see me, so that boosted my ego. We talked about things over pancakes and coffee. I talked some about my father, about working here at the park, and what I should do next. He hates his job and wants to move on, but he doesn't know where to go. He seems unsure of his destiny, worried about taking the wrong path. Through the entire conversation, I wanted to reassure him that everything would work out. Then, Jason suggested we go for an outing, and I accepted.

First, we went for a walk by Yosemite Falls, which he hadn't yet seen up close. I was completely bored with seeing it by now, but it made me very happy to see him happy. He was like a school kid seeing the earth from space. He wanted to know more about everything, so I started using my tour-guide voice. He loved it. As I took him by the base of the Falls, he grabbed my hand and pulled me through the spray.

We took a small hiking tour through the woods and passed by Lehamite Falls, then by the Royal Arch Cascade. I played tour-guide, talking at length about the trees, the wildlife, the vegetation; he absorbed every bit of it. We worked our way up to Mirror Lake and sat for a while, making wishes as we launched a storm of pebbles into the water. We sat and enjoyed how peaceful it was. Occasionally a tourist would come up and take pictures of the lake, then quietly disappear into the woods. We wanted to stay longer, and if we hadn't gotten hungry, I think we would have.

We walked to the Ahwahnee Hotel, ordered food from the Lodge Restaurant, and sat out on the patio and ate. We watched the sun set and then went back to my place for hot cocoa. Being alone in my room with him was nice. I was thinking about sex half the time and found it hard to keep my focus on the conversation. Of course, now that I'm free from the restraints of "observe and record only," I feel a lot closer to him. There are no more journal entries to worry about, so maybe there's no harm in more contact. Later, in my room, he shocked me by suggesting we go camping. We set Tuesday as the day, and honestly, I'm nervous about being alone with him.

How do you study someone so much and then find yourself together with them, alone, in a romantic setting? It would thrill me if he tried something, but I'm a little intimidated.

06/02/00
Reading is making me tired, and my hand is getting sore. Hearing Gina talk about me like this is odd. She always seemed in control, and she intimidated me. How could I intimidate her? If I had been more honest with her then things might have turned out differently.
I've got to put down this pen and rest for a minute.

Gina's journal 05/29/00
Today I had to work and couldn't see Jason. It bothered me. I think I'm getting too attached. I'll call him and see if he wants to go out and get drinks tonight. Maybe a couple of my friends would come with us to Andy's Bar. What is it about him?

Gina's journal 05/30/00

It's early morning, and I had to call Morgan. Something happened to Jason at the bar last night, and it has me on edge. One moment he was sitting beside me, and the next he was standing up beside the booth. It must have been a jump in time. His hands were covering his ears, and he looked like he was in shock.

It reminded me of a situation that happened when we were in training class. The teachers put me in Chamber A and sent me back 5 minutes in the past to Chamber B. After the transfer, I had to stay secluded for 5 minutes so I wouldn't contaminate time. What they didn't tell me was that the power generator was next to Chamber B. As soon as I transferred, the sound inside the chamber nearly made my knees buckle.

Something similar happened to Jason, I'm sure. Morgan says these rogue agents must be creating windows for stopping time and soon they may be able to reach him. Base thinks these other agents are trying to get his journal so that no one in the future finds it. If no one ever finds the notebook then a cascade of events could occur. We might never even create a Base station. Everything we've done would be gone. Morgan said from now on they'll keep a constant watch on Jason in the past, before Yosemite, as well. We had people looking after him, but now an increase is needed to make sure he's not interfered with until the book is completed.

Morgan told me that Base is calculating the risk of having Jason come back with us, but the variables are changing so fast they can't be sure if it's the right option. My opinion is screw the variables and take him out. If my contacting him is recorded in his journal then we are already affecting the future and everything is unchangeable, as Jason might say. I didn't ask Jason what happened last night because I didn't want to upset him more. I just wanted him to feel safe.

When he dropped me off, I wanted to hold him. He looked like he had been really frightened by the experience. I didn't know what to do, so I kissed him. It was just a reaction, and I couldn't have stopped myself if I wanted to, and I didn't want to. How many times did I lay awake wondering if that kiss would happen, and where it might happen: on the Sentinel Bridge, walking by Yosemite Falls, lying under the stars? It wasn't what I had daydreamed about, but it wasn't anything less, either.
I gave him my number in case he needed to call me. We need to get him out of here. I can't stand seeing him used and fought over like this.

We're still on for the campout. I'm nervous!

Gina's journal 05/30/00
Yesterday's experience at the bar with Jason worried me, so I called Morgan once again at the Tuolumne center. Everyone seemed concerned about the time distortions and what it might be doing to him. Morgan said the group is debating evacuating him because of the danger. Until they decide to give me the O.K., I'll have to look after him. These distortions he's experiencing could have been happening for some time now. I wonder if he's been having any other experiences outside the park that we don't know about.

The campout is still on for tonight. I can't think about all these other issues while I'm with Jason. I'll just have to act as if everything is O.K. I didn't want to tell anyone at Base about the campout, but, with these recent problems, I thought it best to mention it. Morgan wasn't exactly happy about it, but he understood and told me not to get eaten by bears.

06/02/00
If I make it to the past then I can change things for Gina. My only hope is to find Morgan. And if I do find him, then I could go back in time and reach Gina. At daybreak I'll leave for the Tuolumne area and start searching for…something.

Gina's journal 05/31/00
It's morning now, and Jason has stepped away from the campsite. How do I tell him I had a crush on him when I was only six years old? There are so many things I want him to know, but I'm not able to say. I almost told him everything last night. When I looked in his eyes, sitting there by the campfire…if he only knew. He inspired me, changed me forever, and I can't even tell him. All the friends I grew up with used to imagine going back in time and meeting him, and now here I am.

Last night we started talking about family conflicts, and I saw a part of him that no one had known. I feel guilty because I started telling him about my life just to open him up, and it worked. It seems our family histories are very similar.

He told me the story I was desperately waiting to hear. The one about him losing his grandfather's ring in the creek. He took the ring one day without thinking. He forgot it was on his finger and went swimming in a nearby creek. He said he felt embarrassed about the two girls sitting on the bank watching him dive over and over again looking for the ring. When I used to read that story I felt so sorry for him.

One day, when Karen and I were in school, we came up with a plan. Her older brother worked the night shift at the lab, and we decided to take a trip back without asking. Everyone was away from the lab at night, and, for several weeks, we played around with the machine trying to find Jason's location at that creek where he was swimming. He didn't give a specific date so it took us a long time, then finally it happened. Karen and I found ourselves on that exact bank of that exact creek where he had lost his ring. We watched him dive frantically, and for an hour, trying to find the ring, but it didn't help. It was so sad, and I knew that we had equipment back at the lab that could find the ring in a minute. So the next night, we went back to the creek and got the ring, but we never told anyone. We were so proud for ourselves, and that we had found the very ring he mentioned early in his journal. Karen and I took turns wearing it to class.

But just as important was finding out that we were the girls he mentioned in his journal. After that, my arguments with my Professor in Time Continuum class were very heated. Now I had proof for my arguments, but I couldn't tell anyone or they would have booted me out of the program.

Everyone back home will be jealous that he told me that story.

06/02/00

Karen is a part of it! I'll have to go over there and talk to her. If she and Gina came here together, then she can help me get back to Gina's time, and the machine. I'll be back shortly.

06/02/00

Karen was still sleeping when I showed up. She was visibly upset about Gina and worried about me. I told her I knew what she and Gina were sent here for. She mentioned that Gina's journal was missing and that the communication link with Base had been broken. I didn't know anything about the communication device, but I kept quiet about the journal. We sat down, and she said I was in trouble and needed to get out of the park within a few hours. I said I wanted to go back with her to the Base, and she agreed. She had not been given authorization to interfere, but said she saw no choice now that Gina was gone.

I asked her if she thought Gina might have been killed. She said rumors had surfaced of an increasing number of operatives in the park.

Someone was onto their plan to get me out of the park and was trying
everything possible to capture me. She said she was a backup in
helping Gina watch out for me. When I told her Gina had mentioned
the story of my ring, she opened a small box and there was the ring that
I'd lost when I was a child. I probably stared at it for several minutes
before I could pick it up. The tape that I'd put on it when I was a child
to help it fit my finger was still there. I unwrapped the tape and slipped
it over my left ring finger, and it fit perfectly. I had just started
wondering what my dad would think when Karen interrupted. She told
me to pack up only my necessities and my journal. She said she would
pick me up at my place at 10:00 AM

As I walked back from Karen's, I saw the beginning of the dawn in the
Valley. The sky was changing from dark blue to shades of orange and
gold. That may have been the last sunrise I'll ever see from here. As I
walked, occasionally I would catch myself glancing down at the ring
on my finger in amazement and smiling. Realizing that this morning's
walk might be the strongest memory of my life, I began to take in the
surroundings as much as possible. The smells and sounds of the woods
were alive, touching the leaves on the trees, feeling the breeze on my
face. The cool air surrounded me. The sun began casting rays of light
from behind a silhouetted mountain. As I crossed one of the meadows,
a deer raised his head and looked at me. Everything was alive again,
and more vibrant than ever before.

I took a short nap when I got back in the room. Now I only have a
short time before Karen gets here. I want to finish copying as much of
Gina's journal as possible.

> Gina's journal 05/31/00
> I've tried not to act odd around Jason because I don't want
> him to know about the situation he's in, but my expressions
> may be giving it away. So far I've kept him safe, but I'm not
> sure how long I can do this. Jason wants to meet me at the
> Mountain Room Bar tonight, so I'm going to call Morgan
> and see if I can tell Jason everything tonight.

Gina's journal 05/31/00

It's almost midnight, and I've just done the irreversible. Earlier, I called Morgan and he asked me to meet him at 7:00 p.m. in Tuolumne. He told me not to let anyone know that I was coming. I thought I could still make my 9:00 date with Jason at the Mountain Room Bar, but Morgan neglected to tell me about the meeting that was waiting for me. Most of the Tuolumne group was there, and some of the staff from the Alpha Base had transported in for this occasion.

Everyone was sitting at the conference table when I walked in, some were smiling, and some were not. As soon as I sat down they began asking me questions about my experiences. I told them everything that they needed to know, but nothing they didn't. They started coming up with a plan. I mentioned my idea about the time continuum, and Jason's entry of "the group." They seemed to be in agreement with me, they had already thought about that and several other things.

At one point I looked over and saw a couple of people glaring at me with a smirk on their face and I got hot. Before I had time to stand up and confront them, Morgan had grabbed my arm. He knows me better than any of them. Morgan told me that everyone was very concerned about Jason. I asked the two "smirks" what the matter was. He said they had just received word that a rogue agent was in the park and might have been there for several days. Before I knew it, I was yelling at my superiors. As soon as I realized it, I took a deep breath and asked why I was called away from the park when he might be in danger. Their rationale was that he would be safe for a short time with Karen nearby. But I still needed to get back to him. Besides, we had a date.

Before they closed the meeting they voiced one more concern. They said with Jason in danger and with no other existing record of him, they saw no reason not to inform him. They said to give him the choice of coming back with me or staying where he is. They decided his disappearance from further record was just as likely due to him coming to the future with me as any other scenario. I felt the blood rush into my cheeks when they told me. I could tell him everything, show him everything that has been done. Seeing his face as he walks through the halls of the Base, unaware 'til then that he has been the inspiration for so many of those who built it.

After more longwinded deliberation they surprised me by concluding that the journal had to stay behind. All along I thought they wanted the notebook, and they did. But they said that without his journal being left behind for us to find, there might be no "us" as we know it, and all the work we've done might be gone. As much as I wanted to know the entire contents of his book too, I agreed with their decision.

I looked at my watch and the time was 10:00 p.m. The meeting ended, and I felt terrible about missing our date. It would take at least an hour to get back to the park, and then where would I find him? When I arrived back in Yosemite Valley it was after 11:00 p.m. The Mountain Room Bar had closed, but I went there anyway just to see if he was sitting outside. He wasn't. I went to his room and knocked on the door, but there was no answer. I wanted to tell him everything so badly that I couldn't wait for morning, so I went down and got some paper and a pen from the office and wrote him a letter. It would have been so wonderful to have said it in person, but I had to warn him of the dangers too. I couldn't chance not telling him. There's the phone!

06/02/00

When I called her, I would never have thought that the next day she would be dead. I didn't know about all the things she was doing for me. The fact that there's now hope of getting back to her helps keep me awake and functioning. It's getting close to 10:00 AM, and Karen should be showing up shortly.

Gina's journal 06/01/00
It's about 3:00 in the morning. Jason called a while ago and said he would come back with me. I'm so happy and so tired. He wanted to know more about me than he did about where he was going. It's overwhelming. I wish I could tell him more, but I've been told not to divulge too much, in case he changes his mind. I'm excited but exhausted. I have to get some sleep.

Gina's journal 06/01/00
Morgan called me this morning and told me some terrible news. Alpha Base called him, and their informants have proof that my roommate Karen is the rogue agent here in the Park. I have got to let Jason know that he's in trouble. He's already gone to mail his book to someone for safe keeping. He's coming back shortly, and I can't find Karen. Why didn't I suspect her? How could she do this? All that time we spent together in school and training? Jason and I must leave as soon as possible, and I can't let Karen get near him.

06/02/00
That was Gina's last entry in her journal! Karen is supposed to be here any minute. I've got to get out of this room.

06/02/00
This will be my last entry. I'm sitting in my Jeep and I'm parked…I won't say where I'm parked. There's no time to go back to the bank and put this book in the safe deposit box. I'll have to put my journal and Gina's in another place. My plan is to make it to Tuolumne and find Morgan. I just bought a map of Tuolumne Meadows and the place is huge. I have no idea where to start. My chances don't look good right now because the time is 10:32, and Karen knows I'm not in my room anymore.

Just in case I don't make it, I want this to be my last wish. Whoever finds this journal please get it into the right hands, preferably someone I've already mentioned here in the journal. I wrote a couple of important phone numbers on a blank page in the back of this notebook. I can't write down where I'm going to put the book, because then the future might find out. As long as these journals are safe, I don't care what happens to me.

I'm putting Gina's journal in a separate location. I just hope that at least one of them, or a copy, survives intact so that I have a chance and Gina has a chance.

I wish I had time to say more, but I don't. Whoever you are please, take care of this book. Let the Fates guide you.